"Is a hundred thousand dollars not enough?" He came closer, his dark eyes bright in the moonlight, the white smoke of his breath drifting around them in the chilly night air. "Let's make it a cool million. A million dollars, Laura. For a single night."

She gasped. *A million…?*

Reaching out, he stroked her cheek. "Think what that money could mean for you. For your family." His fingers moved slowly against her cold skin—the lightest touch of a caress, warming her. "If you don't care what it would mean for me, think what it could do for you. And all you need to do," he said huskily, "is smile for a few hours. Drink champagne. Wear a fancy ball gown. And pretend to love me."

JENNIE LUCAS had a tragic beginning for any would-be writer: a very happy childhood. Her parents owned a bookstore, and she grew up surrounded by books, dreaming about faraway lands. When she was ten, her father secretly paid her a dollar for every classic novel (*Jane Eyre, War and Peace*) that she read.

At fifteen, she went to a Connecticut boarding school on scholarship. She took her first solo trip to Europe at sixteen, then put off college and traveled around the U.S., supporting herself with jobs as diverse as gas-station cashier and newspaper advertising assistant.

At twenty-two, she met the man who would be her husband. For the first time in her life, she wanted to stay in one place, as long as she could be with him. After their marriage, she graduated from Kent State University with a degree in English, and started writing books a year later.

Jennie was a finalist in the Romance Writers of America's Golden Heart contest in 2003 and won the award in 2005. A fellow 2003 finalist, Australian author Trish Morey, read Jennie's writing and told her that she should write for Harlequin® Presents. It seemed like too big a dream, but Jennie took a deep breath and went for it. A year later, Jennie got the magical call from London that turned her into a published author.

Since then, life has been hectic—juggling a writing career, a sexy husband and two young children—but Jennie loves her crazy, chaotic life. Now, if she could only figure out how to pack up her family and live in all the places she's writing about!

For more about Jennie and her books, please visit her website at www.jennielucas.com.

RECKLESS NIGHT IN RIO

JENNIE LUCAS

~ One Night In... ~

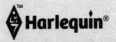
Harlequin®

TORONTO NEW YORK LONDON
AMSTERDAM PARIS SYDNEY HAMBURG
STOCKHOLM ATHENS TOKYO MILAN MADRID
PRAGUE WARSAW BUDAPEST AUCKLAND

Recycling programs
for this product may
not exist in your area.

ISBN-13: 978-0-373-52822-6

RECKLESS NIGHT IN RIO

First North American Publication 2011

Copyright © 2011 by Jennie Lucas

This edition published by arrangement with Harlequin Books S.A.

For questions and comments about the quality of this book please contact us at Customer_eCare@Harlequin.ca.

® and TM are trademarks of the publisher. Trademarks indicated with ® are registered in the United States Patent and Trademark Office, the Canadian Trade Marks Office and in other countries.

www.Harlequin.com

Printed in U.S.A.

RECKLESS NIGHT
IN RIO

To Pete

CHAPTER ONE

"Who is the father of your baby, Laura?"

Holding her six-month-old baby on her hip, Laura Parker had been smiling with pride and pleasure across her family's two-hundred-year-old farmhouse, lit with swaying lights and filled with neighbors and friends for her sister's evening wedding reception. Now, pushing up her black-rimmed glasses, Laura faced her younger sister with a sinking feeling in her heart.

Who is the father of your baby?

People rarely asked that question anymore, since Laura always refused to answer. She'd started to hope the scandal might be over.

"Will you ever tell?" Becky's face was unhappy beneath her veil. At nineteen, her sister was an idealistic new bride with romantic dreams of right and wrong. "Robby deserves a father."

Trying to control the anguish in her heart, Laura kissed her son's dark hair, so soft, and smelling of baby shampoo. She said in a low voice, "We've talked about this."

"Who is he?" her sister cried. "Are you ashamed of him? Why won't you tell?"

"Becky!" Laura glanced uneasily at the reception

guests around them. "I told you... I don't..." She took a deep breath. "I don't know who he is."

Her sister stared at her tearfully. "You're lying. There's no way you'd sleep around like that. You're the one who convinced me to wait for true love!"

The people closest to them had stopped pretending to talk, and were now openly eavesdropping. Family and friends were packed into the farmhouse's warren of rooms, walking across creaking floors, having conversations beneath the low ceilings. Neighbors sat on folding chairs along the walls, holding paper plates of food in their laps. And probably listening. Laura held her baby closer. "Becky, please," she whispered.

"He deserted you. And it's not fair!"

"Becky," their mother said suddenly from behind them, "I don't think you've met your great-aunt Gertrude. She's traveled all the way from England. Won't you come and greet her?" Smiling, Ruth Parker reached for her grandson in Laura's arms. "She'll want to meet Robby, too."

"Thank you," Laura whispered soundlessly to her mother. Ruth answered with a loving smile and a wink, then drew her younger daughter and baby grandson away. Laura watched them go, love choking her. Ruth was wearing her nicest Sunday dress and bright coral lipstick, but her hair had grown gray and her body slightly stooped. The past year had left even her strong mother more frail.

The lump in Laura's throat felt razor-sharp as she stood alone in the crowded room. She'd thought she'd put the scandal of her pregnancy behind her, after she'd returned to her northern New Hampshire village pregnant, with no job and no answers. But would her family ever get over it? Would she?

Three weeks after she'd left Rio de Janeiro, she'd been shocked to discover she was pregnant. Her burly, overprotective father had demanded to know the name of the man. Laura had been afraid he might go after Gabriel Santos with an ultimatum—or worse, a shotgun. So she'd lied and said she had no idea who her baby's father might be. She'd described her time in Rio as one gigantic shagfest, when the truth was that she'd had only one lover her whole life. And even that had been for a single night.

One precious night…

I need you, Laura. She still felt the violence of her boss's embrace as he'd pushed her back against his desk, sweeping aside paperwork and crashing the computer to the floor. After more than a year, she could still feel the heat of his body against hers, the feel of his lips against her neck, his hot brutal kisses against her skin. The memory of the way Gabriel Santos had ruthlessly taken her virginity still invaded her dreams every night.

And the memory of the aftermath still left a shotgun blast in her heart. The morning after he'd seduced her, she'd tearfully told him she felt she had no choice but to quit her job. He'd just shrugged. "Good luck," he said. "I hope you find what you're looking for."

That was all he gave her, after five years of her love and devoted service.

She'd loved her playboy boss, stupidly and without hope. It had been fifteen months since she'd last seen Gabriel's face, but she could not forget it, no matter how hard she tried. How could she, when every day she saw those same dark eyes in her child's face?

Her tears in the little white clapboard church an hour ago hadn't just been from happiness for Becky. Laura had once loved a man with all her heart, but he hadn't loved her back. And as the cold February wind whipped through their northern valley, there were still times she imagined she could hear his dark, deep voice speaking to her, only to her.

"Laura."

Like now. The memory of his low, accented voice seemed so real. The sound ripped through her body, through her heart, as if he were right beside her, whispering against her skin.

"Laura."

His voice felt really close that time.

Really close.

Laura's hands shook as she set down her glass of cheap champagne. Lack of sleep and a surfeit of dreams were causing her to hallucinate. Had to be. It couldn't be…

With a deep breath, she turned.

Gabriel Santos stood before her. In the middle of her family's crowded living room, he towered over other men in every way, even more darkly handsome than she remembered. But it wasn't just his chiseled jawline or his expensive Italian suit that made him stand out. It wasn't just his height or the strength of his broad shoulders.

It was the ruthless intensity of his black eyes. A tremble went through her.

"Gabriel…?" she whispered.

His sensual lips curved. "Hello, Laura."

She swallowed, pressing her nails into her palms, willing herself to wake up from this nightmare—

from this incredible dream. "You can't be here," she whispered. "As in *here*."

"And yet I am," he said. "Laura."

She shivered at the sound of her name on his lips. It didn't seem right that he could be here, in her family's living room, surrounded by friends and family eating potluck.

At thirty-eight, Gabriel Santos owned a vast international conglomerate that bought and shipped steel and timber across the world. His life was filled with one passionate, single-minded pursuit after another. Business. Adrenaline-tinged sports. Beautiful women. Laura's lips turned downward. Beautiful women most of all.

So what was he doing here? What could he possibly have come for unless…unless…

Out of the corner of her eye, she saw her mother disappearing down the hall with her baby.

Trying to stop her hands from shaking, Laura folded her arms around the waist of her hand-sewn bridesmaid's dress. So Gabriel had come to Greenhill Farm. It didn't exactly require a crack team unit to find her here. Parkers had lived here for two hundred years. It didn't mean he knew about Robby. It didn't. He couldn't.

Could he?

Gabriel lifted a dark eyebrow. "Are you glad to see me?"

"Of course I'm not glad." She bit out the words. "If you recall, I'm no longer your secretary. So if you've come five thousand miles because you need me to go back to Rio and sew a button or make your coffee—"

"No." His eyes glittered at her. "That's not why I've come." He slowly looked around the house, which was decorated with strings of pink lights and red paper hearts along the walls, and candles above the fire in the old stone fireplace. "What's going on here?"

"A wedding reception."

He blinked, then came closer to her, the wooden boards creaking beneath his feet. Laura's eyes widened as the shadows of firelight shifted across the hard angles of his face. He was so handsome, she thought in bewildered wonder. She'd forgotten how handsome. Her dreams hadn't done him justice. She could see why so many women chased after him all over the world…and why he was the despair of them all.

"And just who—" his black eyes narrowed into a glower "—is the bride?"

She was bewildered at the sudden harshness of his tone. "My little sister. Becky."

"Ah." His shoulders relaxed imperceptibly. Then he frowned. "Becky? She's not much more than a child."

"Tell me about it." Laura looked down at her bridesmaid's dress. In the gleam of the fire and pink lights swaying above, the pale pink gown appeared almost white. She looked up suddenly. "Did you think it was me?"

Their eyes locked in the crowded room.

"*É claro*," Gabriel said quietly. "Of course I thought it was you."

The idea of her having the time or the interest to date, let alone marry, some other man made her choke back a laugh. She smoothed her bridesmaid's gown with trembling hands. "No."

"So there is no one important in your life right now?" he asked, in a casual tone belied by way he held his body in absolute stillness.

There *was* someone important in her life. She just had

to get Gabriel out of here before he saw Robby. "You have no right to ask."

"*Sim*." He paused. "But you're not wearing a ring."

"Fine." Laura's voice was painfully quiet as she looked down at her feet. "I'm not married."

She didn't have to ask if Gabriel was married. She already knew the answer. How many times had he told her he would never, ever take a wife?

I'm not made for love, querida. *I'll never have a little housewife cooking my dinner in a snug house every night as I read books to our children.*

Gabriel moved closer, almost touching her. She was dimly aware of people whispering around them, wondering who this handsome, well-dressed stranger might be. She knew she should tell him to leave, but she was caught in the power of his body so close to hers. Her gaze fell on his thick wrists beneath sharply tailored shirt cuffs, and she trembled. She remembered the feel of that strong body on hers, the stroke of his fingertips....

"Laura."

Against her will, her eyes lifted, tracing up his muscular body, past his broad shoulders and wide neck to his brutally handsome face. In the flickering shadows, she saw the dark scruff along his jaw, the scar across his temple from a childhood car accident. She saw the man she'd wanted forever and had never stopped wanting.

His eyes burned into her, and memories poured through her. She felt vulnerable, almost powerless beneath the dark fire of his glance.

"It's good to see you again," he said in a low voice. He smiled, and the masculine beauty of his face took her breath away. Their fifteen months apart had made him only more handsome. While she…

She hadn't seen the inside of a beauty salon for a year. Her hair hadn't been cut for ages, and her only makeup was lipstick in an unflattering pink shade that she'd worn at Becky's insistence. Her dowdy dishwater-blonde hair had been hurriedly pulled back in a French knot before the ceremony, but now fell about her shoulders in messy tendrils, pulled out by Robby's chubby fists.

Even as a girl Laura had always tended to put herself last, but since she became the single mother of a baby, she wasn't even on the list. Taking a shower and shoving her hair back into a ponytail was all she could manage most days. And she still hadn't managed to take off all the extra weight from her pregnancy. Nervously, she pushed up her black-framed glasses. "Why are you staring at me?"

"You're even more beautiful than I remembered."

Her cheeks went hot beneath his gaze. "Now I know you're lying."

"It's true." His dark eyes seared her. He wasn't looking at her as if he thought she were plain. In fact, he was looking down at her as if he…

As if he…

He turned away, and she exhaled.

"So this is Becky's wedding reception?" He glanced around the room with something like disapproval on his face.

Laura thought their home looked nice, even romantic for a country-style winter wedding. They'd scrubbed it scrupulously clean, tidied away all the usual clutter, and decorated their hearts out. But as she followed his gaze, she suddenly saw how shabby it all was.

Laura had been proud of how much she'd been able to accomplish for her sister on almost no budget. Flowers had been too expensive because of Valentine's Day, so Laura had gone to the nearest craft store and cut out large hearts of red tissue paper, festooning them on their walls with red and pink balloons and streamers. She'd decorated the house in the middle of the night, as she'd waited for the cake to cool. For the reception dinner, their mother had made her famous roast chickens and their friends and neighbors had brought casseroles and salads for a buffet-style potluck. Laura had made her sister's wedding cake herself, using instructions from an old 1930s family cookbook.

She'd been tired but so happy when she'd fallen into bed at dawn. But now, beneath Gabriel's eyes, the decorations no longer seemed beautiful. She saw how flimsy it all was, how shabby a send-off for her second-youngest sister. Becky had seemed delighted when she saw the decorations and slightly tilted wedding cake that morning. But what else could she have done, knowing how hard her family had tried to give her a nice wedding when there was never a dime to spare?

As if he could read her mind, Gabriel looked at her. "Do you need money, Laura?"

Laura's cheeks went hot. "No," she lied. "We're fine."

He looked around the room again, at the paper plates with the potluck dinner, at her homemade gown, clearly not believing her. He set his jaw. "I'm just surprised your father couldn't do better for Becky. Even if money is tight."

Laura folded her arms, feeling ice in her heart. "He

couldn't," she whispered. "My father died four months ago."

She heard Gabriel's intake of breath. "What?"

"He had a heart attack during harvest. We didn't find him on his tractor until later. When he didn't come home for dinner."

"Oh, Laura." Gabriel took her hand in his own. "I'm sorry."

She felt his sympathy, felt his concern. And she felt the rough warmth of his palm against her own—the touch she'd craved for the past year and all the five years before. Her fingers curled over his as longing blistered her soul.

With an intake of breath she ripped her hand away.

"Thank you," she said, blinking back tears. She'd thought she was done grieving for her father, but she'd spent most of the day with a lump in her throat, watching her uncle walk Becky down the aisle, seeing her mother alone in the pew with tears streaking her powdered face. Laura's father should have been here. "It's been a long winter. Everything fell apart without him. We're just a small farm and always run so lean, one year to the next. With my dad gone, the bank tried to refuse to extend the loan or give us anything more for spring planting."

Gabriel's eyes narrowed. "What?"

She lifted her chin. "We're fine now." Although they were just surviving on fumes, trying to hold on another week until they'd get the next loan. Then they'd pray next year would be better. She folded her arms. "Becky's husband, Tom, will live at the house and farm the land now. Mom will be able to stay in her home and be well looked after."

"And you?" Gabriel asked quietly.

Laura pressed her lips together. Starting tonight, she and Robby were moving into her mother's bedroom. The three-bedroom farmhouse was now full, since Laura and her baby could no longer share a bedroom with Becky, and her other sisters, Hattie and Margaret, shared the other. Ruth had loyally said she'd be delighted to share her large master bedroom with her grandson, but Ruth was a very light sleeper. It was not an ideal situation.

Laura needed a job, an apartment of her own. She was the oldest daughter—twenty-seven years old. She should be helping her family, not the other way around. She'd been looking for a job for months, but there were none to be had. Not even at a fraction of the salary she'd earned when she worked for Gabriel.

But there was no way she was going to tell him that. "You still haven't explained what you're doing here. You obviously didn't know about the wedding. Do you have some kind of business deal? Is it the old Talfax mine that's for sale?"

He shook his head. "I'm still trying to close the Açoazul deal in Brazil." His jaw tightened. "I came because I had no choice."

Over the noisy conversation nearby, Laura heard a guitar and flute play the opening notes of an old English folk song from somewhere in the house. She heard a baby's bright laugh over the music and a chilling fear whipped through her. "What do you mean?"

His dark eyes narrowed. "Can't you guess?"

Laura sucked in her breath. All her worst nightmares were about to come true.

Gabriel had come for her baby.

After all the times he'd said he never wanted a child, after everything he'd done to make sure he'd never be burdened with one, somehow he'd found out Laura's deepest secret and he'd come to take Robby. And he wouldn't even take their son out of love, oh no. He'd do it out of duty. Cold, resentful duty.

"I don't want you here, Gabriel," Laura whispered, trembling. "I want you to leave."

He set his jaw grimly. "I can't."

Ice water flooded her veins as she stood near the fireplace in the warm parlor. "What brought you? Was it some rumor—or…" She licked her lips and suddenly could no longer bear the strain. "For God's sake. Stop toying with me and tell me what you want!"

His dark eyes looked down at her, searing straight through her soul.

"You, Laura," he said in a low voice. "I came for you."

CHAPTER TWO

I came for you.

Stricken, Laura stared up at him with her lips parted.

Gabriel's dark eyes were hot and deep with need. Exactly as he'd looked at her the night he'd taken her virginity. The night she'd conceived their child.

I came for you.

How many times had she dreamed of Gabriel finding her and speaking those words?

She'd missed him constantly over the last fifteen months, as she'd given birth to their baby alone, woken up in the night alone and raised their child without a father. She'd yearned for his strong, protective arms constantly. Especially during the bad times, such as the moment she'd told her family she was pregnant. Or the day of her father's funeral, when her mother and three younger sisters had clung to her, sobbing, expecting her to be the strong one. Or the endless frustrating weeks when Laura had gone to the bank with her baby in tow, day after day, to convince them to extend the loan that would let their farm continue to operate.

But there had been happy times as well, and then she'd missed Gabriel even more. Such as the day halfway into her pregnancy, when she'd been washing dishes in the tiny kitchen and she'd suddenly clutched her curved belly and laughed aloud in wonder as she felt—this time for sure—their baby's first kick inside her. Or the sunny, bright August day when Robby had been born, when she'd held his tiny body against her chest and he'd blinked up at her, yawning sleepily, with dark eyes exactly like his father's.

For over a year, Laura had missed Gabriel like water or sun or air. She'd craved him day and night. She'd missed the sound of his laugh. Their friendship and camaraderie.

And now, he'd finally come for her?

"You came for me?" she whispered. Was it possible he'd thought of her even a fraction of the times her heart had yearned for him? "What do you mean?"

"Just what I said," Gabriel said quietly. "I need you."

She swallowed. "Why?"

His dark eyes glittered in the flickering firelight. "Every other woman has been a pale shadow of you in every way."

If her heart had been fluttering before, now it was frantically rattling against her ribs. Had she been wrong to leave him, fifteen months ago? Had she been wrong to keep Robby a secret? What if Gabriel's feelings had changed, and all this time he'd cared for her? What if—

He leaned forward as his lips curved into a smile. "I need you to come work for me."

Laura's heart stopped, then resumed a slow, sickly beat.

Of course. *Of course* that was all he would want. He'd

likely forgotten their one-night affair long ago, while she
would remember it forever—in her passionate dreams,
in the eyes of their son. Laura stared up at Gabriel's
dark, brutally handsome face. She saw the tension of
his jawline, the taut muscles of his folded arms beneath
his suit jacket.

"You must want it badly," she said slowly.

He gave her a tight smile. "I do."

Out of the corner of her eye, she saw her mother
coming back down the hall, holding Robby in one arm
and a slice of wedding cake in her other hand. Laura
sucked in her breath.

Robby. How could she have allowed herself to forget,
even for an instant, that her son was counting on her to
keep him safe?

Grabbing Gabriel's hand, she pulled him out of the
room, dragging him out of the house, away from prying
eyes and into the freezing February air.

Outside in the wintry night, cars and trucks were
wedged everywhere along the gravel driveway between
their old house and the barn, strewn along the country
road in front of their farm. Across the old stone walls
that lined the road, white rolling hills stretched out into
the great north woods, disappearing now into the falling
purple twilight.

Behind them, next to the old barn, she could see the
frozen water of their pond, gleaming like a silver mirror
under the lowering gray clouds. Her father had taught
all his daughters to swim there during the summers of
their childhood, and even though Laura was now grown,
whenever she felt upset, she would go for a swim in the
pond. Swimming made her think of her father's protective arms. It always made her feel better.

She wished she could swim in the pond now.

Laura looked down at her breath in the chilly air and saw the white smoke of Gabriel's mingle with hers. She realized she was still holding his hand and looked down at his large fingers enfolding her own. The warmth of them suddenly burned her skin, sizzling nerve endings the length of her body.

She dropped his hand. Folding her arms, she glared up at him. "I'm sorry you've come all this way for nothing. I'm not going to work for you."

"You don't even want to hear about the job first? For instance—" he paused "—how much it pays?"

Laura bit her lip, thinking of her bank account, which held exactly thirteen dollars—barely enough for a week's supply of diapers, let alone groceries. But they'd get by. And she couldn't risk Robby's custody—not for something so unimportant as money! She lifted her chin fiercely. "No amount of money could tempt me."

His lips quirked. "I know I wasn't always the easiest man to live with—"

"Easy?" she interjected. "You were a nightmare."

His eyes crinkled in a smile. "Now that's the diplomatic Miss Parker I remember."

She glared at him. "Find another secretary."

"I'm not asking you to be my secretary."

"You said…"

He looked down at her. His voice was dark and deep, his eyes burning though her with intensity. "I want you to spend a night with me in Rio. As my mistress."

His mistress? Laura's mouth fell open.

Gabriel continued to stare down at her with his inscrutable dark eyes, his hands in his pockets. She licked her lips.

"I'm...I'm not for sale," she whispered. "You think just because you are rich and handsome you can have whatever you want, that you can pay me to fall into your bed—and go away the next morning with a check?"

"A charming idea." A humorless smile traced his sensual mouth. "But I don't wish to pay you for sex."

"Oh." Her cheeks went hot. "Then what?"

"I want you—" he moved closer, his hard-edged face impossibly handsome "—to pretend to love me."

She swallowed. Then she tilted her head, blinking up at him in the fading light. "But thousands of girls could do that," she said. "Why come all the way up here, when you could have twenty girls at your penthouse in Rio in four minutes? Are you insane?"

He raked his dark hair back with his hand.

"Yes," he said heavily. "I am going slowly insane. Every moment my father's company is in the hands of another man, every moment I know I lost my family's legacy through my own stupidity, I feel I am losing my mind. I've endured it for almost twenty years. And I'm close now, so close to getting it back."

She should have known it had something to do with regaining Açoazul. "But how can I possibly help you?"

He looked down at her, his jaw clenched. "Play the part of my devoted mistress for twenty-four hours. Until I close the deal."

"How on earth would that help you close the deal?" she asked, bewildered.

He set his jaw. "I've hit a snag in the negotiations. A six-foot-tall, bikini-wearing snag."

"What?"

Gabriel ground his teeth. "Felipe Oliveira found out I used to date his fiancée."

"You did?" Laura said in surprise, then gave a bitter laugh. "Of course you did."

"Now he doesn't want me within a thousand miles of Rio. He thinks if he doesn't sell me the company after all, I'll go back to New York." Gabriel looked at her. "I need to make him understand I'm not interested in his woman."

"That doesn't explain why you'd need *me*. Thousands of women would be happy to pretend to be in love with you. For free." She took a deep breath, clenching her hands at her sides. "Some of them wouldn't even have to pretend!"

He set his jaw. "They won't work."

She exhaled with a flare of her nostrils. "Why?"

"Oliveira's fiancée…is Adriana da Costa."

"Adriana da…" Laura's voice trailed off, her eyes wide.

Adriana da Costa.

Laura could still see those cold, reptilian eyes, that skinny, lanky body. Gabriel had dated the Brazilian supermodel briefly in New York several years ago, while Laura was his live-in personal assistant. She could still hear Adriana's pouting voice. *Why do you keep calling here? Stop calling.*

Find the whiskey, you stupid cow. Gabriel always gets thirsty after sex.

Laura cleared her throat. "Adriana da Costa, the bikini model."

"Yes."

"The one *Celebrity Star* magazine just called the sexiest woman alive."

"She's a selfish narcissist," he said sharply. "And for the short time we were together, she was always insecure. Only one woman has ever made her feel so threatened. You."

"Me?" Laura gasped. "You're out of your mind! She would never feel threatened by me!"

Gabriel's dark eyes gleamed. "She complained to me constantly. Why did I always take your calls, but not hers? Why did I always have time for you, day or night? Why would I leave her bed at 2:00 A.M. in order to go home to you? And most of all, why did I allow you to live in my apartment, only you and no one else?"

Laura's mouth fell open.

"She never understood our relationship," Gabriel said. "How we could be so close without being lovers. Which we weren't." He paused. "Not until…Rio."

The huskiness of his deep voice whipped through Laura, causing a sizzle to spread down her body.

"Adriana has made it clear she wants me back," he said in a low voice. "She'd leave Felipe Oliveira in an instant for me, and he knows it. Only one thing will convince them both I am not interested in her."

Laura stared at him.

"Me?" she whispered.

He looked right at her. "You are the only woman that Adriana would believe I could love."

A roar of shared memories left unspoken between them washed over Laura like a wave, and her heart twisted in her chest. She'd been only twenty-one when, on her second day in New York City, the employment office had sent her to Santos Enterprises to interview in the accounting office. Instead, she'd been sent up to the top floor to meet with the CEO himself.

"Perfeito," the fearsome, sleek Brazilian tycoon had said, looking at her résumé. Then he'd looked at her. "Young enough so you will not be planning to immediately quit to have a baby. At least ten or twenty years before you'll think of that. *Perfeito.*"

Now, Gabriel looked at her with dark eyes. She felt a cold winter wind sweep in from the north and shivered.

"Be my pretend mistress in Rio," he said. "And I will pay you a hundred thousand dollars for that one night."

Her lips parted as she breathed, "A hundred thousand!"

She almost said yes on the spot. Then she remembered her baby, and her heart rose to her throat. She shook her head. "Sorry," she choked out. "Get someone else."

His brow furrowed in disbelief. "Why? You clearly need the money."

She licked her lips. "That's none of your business."

"I deserve an answer."

She set her jaw. He didn't know what kind of trouble he'd made for her by coming here. *Didn't know and didn't care.* He couldn't see how Laura had changed through the anguish of the past year. Who would be the first neighbor to gossip that her ex-boss bore an uncanny resemblance to her son?

She exhaled, clenching her hands. He still thought all he had to do was tell her to jump, and she'd ask how high. But she wasn't his obedient little secretary anymore.

With a deep breath, she closed her eyes. It was time to let it all go.

Let go the sound of Gabriel's warm, deep voice for the last five years as his executive assistant. *Miss Parker, there's no one as capable as you.*

Let go the brightness of his delight when he came home at 6:00 A.M. to find her silently waiting with freshly made coffee and a pressed suit for his early meeting. *Miss Parker, what would I do without you?*

Let go the memory of their time in bed, when his dark eyes, so vulnerable and warm, had caressed her face with unspoken words of love. Let go the memory of his lips hot against her skin. Let go the feel of him inside her. *Laura, I need you.*

She opened her eyes.

"I'm sorry," she said, her voice shaking. "You don't deserve an explanation. My answer is just no."

Around them, the dusting of snow reflected light into the white-gray lowering clouds, in a breathless hush of muffled silence. He blinked, looking bewildered.

"Did it end so badly, Laura?" he said softly. "Between us?"

She pressed her fingernails into her palms to keep from crying. Robby. She had to think of Robby. "You shouldn't have come here." Her cheeks felt inflamed in the winter air, her body burning up and yet cold as ice. "I want you to leave. Now."

He took a step closer, looking down at her. A sliver of moonlight pierced through the clouds to illuminate his face. She noticed the dark shadow on his hard jawline, saw the hollows beneath his eyes. She wondered when he'd last slept.

Her heart twisted in her chest. No. She couldn't let

herself care. She couldn't! Choking back tears, she edged away. "If you won't leave, I will."

He grabbed her wrist. He looked down at her, and his eyes glittered. "I can't let you go."

For a moment, she heard only the panting of their breath. Then a door banged open, and she heard a baby's whine. A chill went down her spine and she whirled around with a gasp.

Too late!

"Where have you been, Laura?" her mother called irritably, holding a squirming Robby in her arms. "It took me ages to find you. What on earth are you doing out here in the cold?"

Ripping her arm from Gabriel's grasp, Laura gave her mother a hard, desperate stare. "I'm sorry, Mom. Just go back inside. Go back. I'll be right there!"

But her mother wasn't looking at her. "Is that—is that Mr. Santos?" she said tremulously.

"Hello, Mrs. Parker," Gabriel said, smiling as he stepped towards her and held out his hand. "Congratulations on Becky's wedding. You must be very proud of your daughter."

"I'm proud of all my daughters." She came closer to shake his hand. "It's nice to see you again."

Laura stared at them, her heart in her throat. Her mother had always liked Gabriel, ever since he'd paid for the family to take a vacation to Florida four years ago, one they wouldn't otherwise have been able to afford. The Parkers had traveled in his private jet and stayed at a villa on the beach. It had been a lavish second honeymoon for Laura's parents, a big change from their first at a cheap motel in Niagara Falls. Pictures of that Florida vacation still lined the walls, images of their family smiling beneath palm trees, building sand castles on the beach, splashing in the surf together. With that one gift, Gabriel had won her mother's loyalty forever.

"I'm glad someone had the sense to invite you to Becky's wedding," Ruth said, smiling.

He smiled back with gentle courtesy. "I've always asked you to call me Gabriel."

"Oh no, I couldn't," she said. "Not with you being Laura's employer and all. It just wouldn't be right."

"But I'm not her employer anymore." He flashed Laura a dark look before leaning toward her mother to confidentially whisper, "And I wasn't invited to the wedding. I crashed. I came to offer her a job."

"Oh!" Ruth practically cried tears of joy. "A job! You have no idea how happy that makes me. Things have been so tight lately and you should see some of the ridiculous jobs she's applied for, as far away as Exeter—"

"Mom," Laura cried. "Please take Robby inside!"

"So she's looking for a job, is she?" he purred.

"Oh, yes. She's totally broke," Ruth confided, then her cheeks turned red. "But then, we all are. Ever since… since…" She turned away.

Gabriel put his hands into his pockets. "I was sorry to hear about your husband. He was a good man."

"Thank you," Ruth whispered. Amid the lightly falling snow, silence fell. Gabriel suddenly looked at Robby.

"What a charming baby," he murmured, changing the subject. "Is he related to you, Mrs. Parker?"

Her mother looked at him as if he was stupid. "He's my grandson."

Gabriel looked surprised. "Is one of your other daughters married, as well?"

"Mom," Laura breathed with tears in her eyes, terrified, "just go! Right now!"

But it was too late. "This is Robby," her mother said, holding him up proudly. "Laura's baby."

CHAPTER THREE

As her mother turned to place Robby into her arms, Laura's heart fell to the snowy, frozen ground. The six-month-old's whine faded, turning to hiccups as he clung to Laura. Ruth leaned forward to hug her.

"Take the job," her mother whispered in her ear, then turned to Gabriel and said brightly, "I hope to see you again soon, Mr. Santos!"

Laura heard the dull thunk of the door as her mother went back inside. Then she was alone with Gabriel; their baby in her arms.

Gabriel's dark eyes went to the child, then back to her. The sound of his tightly coiled voice reverberated in the cold air. "This is your son?"

She held her baby close, loving the solid, chubby feel of him in her arms. Tears stung her eyes as she looked down at Robby. "Yes."

"How old is he?"

"Six months," she said in a small voice.

Gabriel's eyes narrowed. "So tell me." His voice was deadly and still as a winter's night. "Who is the father of your baby?"

She'd wished so many times to be able to tell Gabriel the truth, dreamed of giving her son his father. With their baby squirming in her arms between them, the truth rose unbidden to her lips. "The father of my baby is…"

You. You're Robby's father. Robby is your son. But the words stuck in her throat. Gabriel didn't want to be tied down with a child. If she told him her secret, nothing good would come of it. He might feel he had no choice but to sue for custody out of duty, resenting Robby, resenting her for forcing him into it. He might try to take their child to Brazil, away from her, to be given into the arms of some young, sexy nanny.

Laura would gain nothing by telling him. And risk everything.

"Well?" he demanded.

She flashed her eyes at him. "The identity of my baby's father is none of your business."

His own eyes narrowed. "You must have gotten pregnant immediately after you left Rio."

"Yes," she said unwillingly. She shivered, looking from father to son. Would he notice the resemblance?

But Gabriel turned on her, his dark eyes full of accusation. "You were a virgin when I seduced you. You said you wanted a home and family of your own. How could you be so careless, to forget protection, to let yourself get pregnant by a one-night stand?"

Gabriel had used protection, but somehow she'd gotten pregnant anyway. She said over the lump in her throat, "Accidents happen."

"Accidents *don't* happen," he corrected. "Only mistakes."

She set her jaw. "My baby is not a *mistake*."

"You mean it was planned?" He lifted a sardonic eyebrow. "Who is the father? Some good-looking farmer?

Some boy you knew back in high school?" He glanced around. "Where is this paragon? Why hasn't he proposed? Why aren't you his wife?"

Robby was starting to snuffle. Even in his long-sleeved shirt, he was getting cold, and so was she. Holding him close to her warmth, she shifted his weight on her hip. "I told you, it's none of your business."

"Is he here?"

"No!"

"So he deserted you."

"I didn't give him the chance," she said. "I left him first."

"Ah." Gabriel's shoulders seemed to relax slightly. "So you don't love him. Will he cause any trouble when you take the child to Rio?"

"No."

"Good."

"I mean—I'm not taking Robby there. I'm not going." Her baby started to whimper as she turned away. "Goodbye, Gabriel."

"Wait."

The raw emotion in his voice made her hesitate. Against her better judgment she turned back. He stepped toward her, and she saw something in his expression she'd never seen before.

Vulnerability.

"Don't leave," he said in a low voice. "I need you."

I need you.

She'd once loved him. She'd served him night and day, existed only to please him. She had to fight that habit, that yearning, with every bit of willpower she possessed.

"Is a hundred thousand dollars not enough?" He

came closer, his dark eyes bright in the moonlight, the white smoke of his breath drifting around them in the chilly night air. "Let's make it a cool million. A million dollars, Laura. For a single night."

She gasped. *A million…?*

Reaching out, he stroked her cheek. "Think what that money could mean for you. For your family." His fingers moved slowly against her cold skin, the lightest touch of a caress, warming her. "If you don't care what it would mean for me, think what it could do for you. And all you need to do," he said huskily, "is smile for a few hours. Drink champagne. Wear a fancy ball gown. And pretend to love me."

Pretend. Blinking up at him, she swallowed the lump in her throat. *Pretend* to love him.

"Although I know it might not be easy," he said dryly. Then he shook his head. "But you are not so selfish as to refuse."

With an intake of breath, Laura clenched her hands into fists. "Maybe I am. Now."

His sensual mouth curved. "The Laura I knew always put the needs of the people she loved above herself. I know that hasn't changed." His dark eyebrow lifted. "You probably stayed up all night making your sister's wedding cake."

Her lips twisted with a dark emotion. "I really hate you."

"Hate me if you will. But if you do not come with me to Rio tonight…" He clawed his black hair back with his hand, then exhaled. His dark eyes seemed fathomless and deep, echoing with pain. "I will lose my father's legacy. Forever."

Shivering in the cold night, cradling her whimpering baby in the warmth of her arms, Laura looked up into Gabriel's handsome, haggard face. She knew better than anyone what the Açoazul company meant to Gabriel. For years, she'd watched him scheme and plot to regain control of it. He hungered for it. *His legacy.*

Living in the house her great-great-great-great-grandfather had built with his own two hands, on the land her family had farmed for two centuries, Laura could understand the feeling. She looked at his face. It was a shock to see raw vulnerability in his dark eyes. It was an expression she'd never seen there before, not in all the years she'd worked for him. She could feel herself weakening.

One million dollars. For a single night of luxury in Rio, a night of beauty and pleasure. She looked down at her baby. What could that money do for her son? For her family?

But oh, the risk. Could she be strong enough to resist telling Gabriel the truth? For twenty-four hours, could she lie to his face? Could she pretend to love him, without falling in love with him again for real?

On the country road in front of their property, Laura saw a parked black sedan turn on its headlights, as if on cue. She heard the smooth purr of the engine as it slowly drove up the driveway. Over Gabriel's head, moonlight laced the ridges of the dark clouds with silver.

She closed her eyes. "You will never come back looking for me after this?" she said in a low voice. "You will leave us in peace?"

Gabriel's own voice was harsh. "Yes."

Looking at him, Laura took a deep breath and spoke

words that felt like a knife between her shoulder blades. The only words he'd left for her to say.

"One night," she whispered.

An hour later they arrived at the small private airport, where his jet waited outside the hangar. As they crossed the tarmac, Gabriel felt his blood rush in his ears as he stared down at her.

Laura was even more beautiful than he remembered. In the moonlight, her hair looked like dark honey. The frosty winter air gave her cheeks a soft pink glow, and as she bit her lower lip, her heart-shaped mouth looked red and inviting. For a single instant, when he'd first seen her at the farmhouse, he'd had the insane desire to kiss her.

He took a deep breath. He was tired, flying straight from Rio on his private jet. Even more than that, he was exhausted from the months of negotiations to buy back his father's old company in Rio, to gain back the business that had been his birthright before he'd stupidly thrown it away as a grief-stricken nineteen-year-old.

He wouldn't fail. Not this time. Gabriel glanced down grimly at his expensive platinum watch. They were still on schedule. *Just.*

As they climbed the steps to the jet, Laura paused, looking behind her. Shifting the baby carrier on her arm, she pulled her diaper bag up higher on her other shoulder and bit her lip. "I think we should go back to the house for a few more things—"

"You have enough for the flight?" he said shortly.

"Yes, but I didn't pack clothes. Pajamas—"

"Everything you need will be waiting for you in Rio. It will be arranged."

"All right." With one last, troubled glance, she followed him up the steps.

Inside the cabin, Gabriel sat down in the white leather seat. A flight attendant offered him a glass of champagne, which he accepted. It had been harder than he'd expected to convince Laura to come. She sat across from him, suddenly glaring at him beneath her dark lashes.

Was she angry at him for some reason? God knew why. He was the one who should be angry. She'd left him in the lurch a year ago. In an act of pure charity, he'd allowed her to quit her job. It had been the act of a saint. He'd barely managed to patch up the hole she'd left in his office.

"You'd better have a very trustworthy babysitter in Rio," she growled, refusing the offer of champagne.

He finished off the crystal flute. "Maria Silva."

She blinked. "Your housekeeper?"

"She was my nanny when I was young."

"You were young?" Laura said sardonically.

Gabriel's throat closed. Against his will, memories of his happy childhood washed over him, of playing with his older brother, of the wrestling and fighting, of his nanny's voice soothing them. Only a year apart in age, Gabriel had competed with Guilherme constantly, always seeking to best him in their parents' eyes. He'd started some stupid battles. Leading up to the night of the accident…

Turning away, he finished harshly, "I'd trust Maria with my life."

Laura no longer looked angry. Now she looked bemused, staring at him with her large, limpid turquoise eyes. She started to ask a question, then was distracted when the flight attendant suggested she buckle in the baby's carrier before takeoff.

Gabriel watched her smiling down at her son, murmuring soft words of love as she tucked a baby blanket into his pudgy hand. The little one yawned again.

A strange feeling went through Gabriel.

He'd won. He'd convinced her. They would make it back to Rio in time. His plan would work. He should be feeling triumphant.

Instead, he felt...on edge.

Why? It couldn't be the money he'd promised her. A million dollars was nothing. He would have paid ten times that to win back his father's company. He would have given every penny he possessed, every share of stock in Santos Enterprises, the contracts, the office building in Manhattan, the ships in Rotterdam. Everything down to the last stick of furniture.

So it wasn't the money. But as the jet took off, leaving New Hampshire behind, he looked out the window. Something bothered him, and he didn't know what it was. Was it that he'd let Laura see his desperation?

No, he thought, setting his jaw. She knew how much his father's company meant to him. And anyway, allowing his vulnerability to show had helped achieve his goal.

It was something else. His gaze settled on the drowsing baby's dark hair, his plump cheeks.

It was the baby. The baby unsettled him.

Gabriel's jaw set as he realized what the edgy feeling was. What it had to be.

Anger.

He couldn't believe that Laura had fallen into another man's bed so swiftly. When she'd quit her job and walked out of his life last year, he'd let her go for one reason only—for her own good. He'd come to care for her. And he knew he couldn't give her what she wanted. A husband. Children. A job that didn't consume her every waking hour. When, the morning after he'd seduced her, she'd suddenly said she was quitting and going back to her family, he'd given Laura her chance at happiness. He'd let her go.

But instead of following her dreams, she'd apparently jumped into a brief, meaningless affair with some man she didn't even care about. She'd settled for poverty and the life of a single mother. She'd allowed her child to be born without a father. Without a name.

Cold rage slowly built inside him.

He'd let her go for nothing.

Gabriel looked at her, now leaning back in her white leather seat with her eyes closed, one hand still on her baby in the seat beside her. She was even more beautiful than he remembered. Even in that unflattering, pale pink satin dress, with that horrible hot pink lipstick, her natural beauty shone through. With all its deceptive innocence.

Against his will, his eyes traced the generous curves beneath her gown. Her breasts were bigger since she'd become a mother, her hips wider. And suddenly he couldn't stop wondering what her body would look like beneath that dress. *What it would feel like against him in bed.*

Erotic memories flashed through him of the first time he'd kissed her, when he'd swept his laptop to the floor in his ruthless need to have her. Taking her against his desk, he'd lost data that had cost thousands of dollars.

He hadn't cared. It had been worth it.

He'd wanted Laura Parker from the moment she'd walked into his office, looking uncertain in her country clothes and wearing big, ugly glasses. He'd seen at once that she had a kind, innocent heart, coupled with the fearless bluntness he needed in an executive assistant. He'd wanted her, but for five years, he'd held himself in check. He needed her too badly in his office, needed her expertise to keep Santos Enterprises—and his life— running like a well-oiled machine. And he knew an old-fashioned woman like Laura Parker would never settle for what a man like Gabriel could offer—money, glamour, an emotionless affair. So he hadn't allowed himself to touch her. Not even to flirt with her.

Until…

Last year, during a helicopter flight from Açoazul's steel factory to the north of the city, Gabriel had looked up from a report to discover his pilot had flown them right over the sharp stretch of road where his family had died nearly twenty years before.

Gabriel had said nothing to the pilot. He'd told himself he felt nothing. Then he'd gone back to the office. It was late, and all his other employees were gone. He'd seen Laura Parker alone at his desk, filing papers in her prim collared shirt and tweed skirt, and something inside him had snapped. Five years of frustrated need had exploded and he'd seized her. Her blue eyes had widened behind her sleek, black-framed glasses as, without a word, he'd ruthlessly kissed her.

That night, he'd discovered two things that shocked him.

First: Miss Parker was a virgin.

Second: beneath her demure exterior, she'd burned him to ashes with her passionate fire.

He'd made love to her roughly against the desk. He'd been more gentle the second time, after they'd taken the elevator up to his penthouse and he'd kissed her for hours, lying across his big bed. The night had been… amazing. More than amazing. It had been the most incredible sexual experience of his life.

Now, looking at her, a cold knot tightened in Gabriel's chest. He'd given that up, and she'd just thrown herself away. She'd let some unworthy man touch her. Get her pregnant with his child.

Gabriel's hands tightened into fists. Perhaps it was hypocritical to feel so betrayed, since he'd enjoyed many women the past year since she'd deserted him. But *enjoy* was not the right word. All Gabriel had done was prove to himself, over and over, that no other woman could satisfy him as Laura had.

Turning away, he set his jaw. He'd get control of Açoazul SA and then send Laura and her baby back to New Hampshire. He'd thought he might ask her to stay in Rio after the deal was done, but now that was impossible. As much as he missed her in the office—as much as he missed her in his bed—he couldn't take her back now. Not now that she had a child.

He couldn't let himself feel, not even for a moment, as if he were part of a family.

"You look tired," he heard Laura say quietly.

He turned to her, and their eyes locked in the semi-darkness of the jet. "I'm fine."

"You don't seem fine."

"A lot has changed." He looked from her to the sleeping baby. He wanted to ask her again who the baby's father was. He wanted to ask how long she'd waited before she'd jumped into bed with a stranger. A week?

A day? What had the man done to seduce her? Bought her some cheap flowers and wine? Given her cheap promises?

What had it taken for the man to convince Laura to surrender the life she'd yearned for, and accept instead just the crumbs of her childhood dreams?

"Gabriel?"

He looked up to find her anxious eyes watching him. "What?"

"What will happen after we arrive in Rio?"

He leaned back in his seat, folding his arms. "Oliveira is hosting an afternoon pool party at his beachside mansion on the Costa do Sul. Adriana will be there."

Laura bit her lip, looking nervous. "Pool party? Like with a swimsuit?"

"And after that," he continued ruthlessly, "you will attend the Fantasy Ball with me."

"Fantasy, huh?" Her full lips twisted. "I hope Brazilian shopping malls sell magic fairy dust, 'cause that's the only thing that will convince anyone I can compete with Adriana da Costa."

"The first person you must convince is yourself," he said harshly. "Your lack of confidence is not attractive. No one will believe I'd be in love with a woman who disappears in the background like a wallflower."

He had the hollow satisfaction of seeing the light in her beautiful face fade. "I just meant…"

"We made a deal. I am paying you well. For the next twenty-four hours, Laura, you will be the woman I need you to be. You belong to me."

Her eyes narrowed with anger and resentment, and as she turned away, some part of him was glad he'd hurt her. He heard the soft snuffle of the baby's breath, and it was like a razor against his throat.

He'd once been comforted by the thought of Laura back at home with her family, following her dreams. Now she'd taken that from him. She'd betrayed him.

And he hated her for that.

CHAPTER FOUR

As they descended through the clouds toward Rio de Janeiro, Laura stared out the porthole window at the city shining like a jewel on the sea. She folded her arms with a huff of breath, still furious.

You belong to me.

Her hands gripped her seat belt. Looking past Robby's baby seat, where he was thankfully sleeping again after a fairly rough night, Laura glanced at Gabriel on the opposite side of the jet. She allowed herself a grim smile.

Poor Robby had been crying half the flight. Gabriel must have been gnashing his teeth to be trapped in his private jet with a baby. Karma, she thought with a degree of satisfaction. Folding her arms, she turned back to the window to see the beautiful, exotic city as they descended through the clouds.

It had been difficult for her to leave her mother and sisters in the middle of Becky's reception. But instead of being angry, her mother and sisters had seemed pleased. They'd hugged her goodbye for the quick weekend trip. "You were so happy working for him once," her mother had whispered. "This will be a new start for you and Robby. I can feel it. It's fate."

Fate.

Laura had barely gotten on this jet before he'd insulted her. Now, he glared at her as if she were a stranger. No, worse than a stranger. He stared at her as if she were scum beneath his feet.

As the jet finally landed at the private airport, her hands gripped the leather armrest. She would never again feel guilty about keeping their baby a secret from Gabriel. After this, she would never let herself feel *anything* for him. She would do her job, pretend to be his adoring mistress—ha!—then collect the check and forget his existence. She *would*.

As the door of the private jet opened, Robby woke up with one of his adorable baby smiles. His toothless grin and happy cooing were worth any amount of sleepless nights, she thought.

"We're just here for one night, Robby," she told her baby, kissing his forehead as she unbuckled his seat. "Just a quick night here and we'll go straight back home."

"Did he sleep well?" Gabriel said sardonically behind her.

She gave him a pleasant answering smile. "Did you?"

As they stepped out of the jet, Rio's sultry heat hit her at once. She went down the steps, blinking in the blinding sunlight and breathing in the scents of tropical flowers, exotic spice and tangy salt from the sea. Lush, white-hot Brazil was the other side of the world from the frigid February weather she'd left behind her.

Looking across the tarmac, Laura saw a waiting white limousine and snorted. The other side of the world? This was a different world entirely!

"*Bom dia*, Miss Parker," the driver said, tipping his hat as he opened the door. "I am glad to see you again. And what's this?" He tickled beneath Robby's chin. "We have a new passenger!"

"*Obrigada*, Carlos," Laura said, smiling. "This is my son, Robby."

"Is the penthouse ready?" Gabriel growled behind them.

The driver nodded. "*Sim, senhor.* Maria, she has organized everything."

"Good."

Laura climbed into the backseat and tucked Robby into the waiting baby seat, ignoring Gabriel climbing in beside him. Carlos started the engine and pulled the limo off the tarmac, going south.

As they traveled through the city, now crowded with tourists for the celebration of *Carnaval*, Laura stared out bleakly at the festive decorations. Gabriel didn't speak and neither did she. The silence seemed like agony as the car inched through the traffic. As they finally approached the back of Gabriel's building, Laura heard loud thumping music, drums, people singing and cheering.

"This is as close as I can get, *senhor*," Carlos said apologetically. "The *avenida* is closed to cars today."

"*Está bom.*" Setting his jaw, Gabriel opened the door himself and got out of the limo.

Laura looked out her window in awe. Ahead of them, she saw the street blocked and people gathering on Ipanema Beach for one of the largest, wildest street festivals in Rio. She looked up at Gabriel's tall building above them. He had bought it two years ago, as a foothold in Rio while he wrestled his father's company back from Felipe Oliveira. The ground floors held restaurants and retail space. The middle floors held the South American offices of Santos Enterprises, still officially headquartered in New York. The top two floors of the building were apartments for his bodyguards, household staff and Maria. The penthouse was, of course, for Gabriel—and, the last time she'd been here, for Laura. She swallowed. She'd never thought she'd be back here.

Especially not with a secret. *A baby.*

The car door wrenched open. She looked up, expecting Carlos, but it was Gabriel. To her shock, the expression on his handsome face was suddenly tender and adoring. His eyes shone with passion and desire.

"At last you are home, *querida,*" Gabriel murmured. He held out his hand. "Home where you belong. It nearly killed me when you left. I never stopped loving you, Laura."

She gasped.

Suddenly she could no longer feel the hot sun blazing overhead or the fresh breeze off the sea. Loud music, horns and drumming and singing from Ipanema Beach all faded into the background. Her heart thrummed wildly in her throat.

Gabriel's black eyes sizzled as he looked down at her, catching up her soul, collecting her like a butterfly in a net.

Then he dropped his hand with a sardonic laugh. "Just practicing."

Setting her jaw, she glared at him. "A million dollars is almost not enough to deal with this," she muttered.

His lip twisted. "Too late to renegotiate."

"Go to hell."

"Is that any way to speak in front of your baby?"

Turning back into the car, Laura unbuckled Robby. Her son cooed happily, reaching up his chubby arms for her embrace, and she was happy she had one person in Brazil who actually loved her. Leaving the baby carrier in the limo, she scooped him out of his seat. He giggled, clinging to her wrinkled satin bridesmaid's dress.

Laura felt tired, grungy, dirty. After her poor night's sleep on the jet, after traveling halfway around the world, and most of all, after the constant friction of having Gabriel near her, Laura's emotions were too close to the surface. The flash of his dark eyes, the slightest touch of his hand, the merest word of kindness from his sensual lips, still made her tremble and melt.

He was poison for her, she thought grimly. Poison wrapped in honeyed words and hot desire.

She held her baby close and walked around Gabriel with as much dignity as she possessed, her shoulders straight. Her pink high heels—picked out from a thrift shop by Becky for five dollars—clattered against the marble floor as Laura walked through the back entrance and past the security guards toward the private elevator.

Gabriel followed her without a word. The elevator doors closed behind them, and she breathed in his scent. She felt his warmth beside her. She didn't look at him. His tall, powerful body was so close and she felt every inch.

The last time they'd been together in this elevator, they'd been on the way to the penthouse, after they'd just made love downstairs on the desk in his office. It had been her first time. He'd been shocked she was a virgin, even apologetic. He'd kissed her so tenderly in this very elevator, taking her back up to the penthouse with whispered promises that this time would be different, that he'd make it good for her, that he'd make her weep with joy.

And he had.

The elevator dinged at the same instant Robby struggled in her arms with a plaintive whine. Looking down, Laura saw he was peeking behind her at Gabriel, reaching out his plump arms. Gabriel didn't move to take the baby, or even smile. Of course he wouldn't. Why would he take the slightest interest in his own child? She knew she was being unreasonable, but she still felt angry. Exhaling, Laura walked into the penthouse.

His modern, masculine, clutter-free apartment had two bedrooms, a study, a dining room and main room off the kitchen. The whole place had clean lines, white walls and high ceilings, and a stark decor. A wall of windows two stories high showcased the breathtaking view of the pool and terrace, with Ipanema Beach and the Atlantic visible beyond.

"I'm so glad to see you again, Senhora Laura." Maria Silva, Gabriel's housekeeper and former nanny, was waiting for them. Her gaze moved to Robby. "This must be your sweet baby."

"*Senhora*?" Laura repeated, confused at how she'd just gotten promoted to a married woman.

The plump-cheeked, white-haired woman blushed. "You're a mother. You deserve respect," she said, then held out her hands to the baby. Robby gave a gleeful cackle, and Maria took him happily in her arms.

Frowning, Laura slowly looked around her. The penthouse seemed the same, but it had changed somehow. She saw to her surprise that all the electric plugs and sharp edges had been covered. Peeking into the dining room, she saw it was entirely filled with toys.

Laura turned to Gabriel in wonder. "All this?" she said. "For one night?"

He shrugged. "Don't thank me. Maria did it."

Laura's heart, which had been rising, fell back to her shoes.

"We'll have a wonderful time this afternoon, won't we?" Maria said to Robby, whirling the baby around to make him giggle. "If you need us, Mrs. Laura, we'll be making lunch."

Laura turned to follow them into the kitchen, but Gabriel stopped her. "They'll be fine. Go freshen up."

She scowled at him. "Stop barking orders at me. You weren't this bad when I worked for you."

"Do you want a shower or not?"

From the kitchen, Laura dimly heard Maria getting out pots and pans as she sang a song to the baby in Portuguese. Robby started banging the pans with a wooden spoon, keeping the beat. They seemed fine. Laura set her jaw, then grudgingly admitted, "I do want a shower."

"You have ten minutes." When she didn't move, he lifted a sardonic eyebrow. "Need help?"

She saw his lips curve as he turned away, walking down the hallway. Pulling off his shirt, he dropped it to the floor as he stopped in the doorway of his bedroom. He looked back at her with heavy-lidded eyes. "Go. Right now. Or I will assist you."

"I'm going!" With a gulp, Laura ran for the safety of her old bedroom.

Her room had changed, as well. All the old furniture she'd had as his live-in secretary was gone, of course.

The space had been turned into a bland guest room. Except…

She saw the brand-new elliptical wooden crib beside the bed, the changing table with diapers and baby clothes and everything else Robby might need. She exclaimed with delight as she touched the smooth wood. In the closet, she saw new clothes for her, as well. Gabriel had truly thought of everything. Going to the closet, she touched a black dress with a soft, satisfied sigh.

Then she saw the size on the tag.

Well, she thought with dismay, he hadn't thought of *everything*.

CHAPTER FIVE

TEN MINUTES LATER, Gabriel paced beneath the hot sun across his rooftop terrace. He stopped, staring down at Ipanema Beach across the Avenida Vieira Souto. He could hear the loud music from the crowds celebrating below. Lifting his eyes, he looked past the throngs of people, past the yellow umbrellas and food vendors to the shining waves of the surf, trying to calm his pounding heart.

Now Laura was here, everything would soon be sorted out. Oliveira and Adriana would both believe that they were in love. They had to believe. Otherwise….

No, he wouldn't let himself think about failure, not even for an instant. He couldn't lose his father's company, not now that it was finally within his grasp. He gripped the railing, glaring at the bright horizon of blue ocean. All along the coastline, tall buildings vied with the sharp green mountains for domination of the sky.

He'd changed into khaki shorts and an open, button-down shirt over a tank top, with flip-flops on his feet, Carioca-style. He paced his private rooftop. Bright sunlight reflected prisms from the water of his swimming pool. Turning back, he stared down blindly at the scantily clad women on Ipanema Beach, to Leblon to the west, ending in the stark, sharp green mountain of Dois Irmãos.

Gabriel had been only nineteen when he'd lost everything. His parents. His brother. His home. His hands tightened on the rail. When he'd had the chance to sell his family's business the day after the funeral, Gabriel had taken it. He'd fled to New York, leaving his grief behind.

Except grief had followed him. Consumed him. Even as he created an international company far larger than his father's had ever been, the guilt of what he'd done—causing the accident, but being the only survivor; inheriting his father's company, only to carelessly sell it—never left him. Never.

"Well, I did it," Laura gasped suddenly behind him. "Ten minutes."

"Very efficient," he said, turning to face her. "You should know that—"

His words froze in his throat.

Gabriel's eyes traced over her in shock as he watched her towel off her long wet hair. He took in the erotic vision of her obscenely full breasts overflowing the neckline of her black dress. He couldn't look away from the fabric outlining her full buttocks and hips.

"Where," he choked out, "did you get that dress?"

She stopped toweling her hair to look at him, tilting her head with a frown. "It was in the closet. Wasn't it for me?"

"Yes." He couldn't stop his gaze from devouring her curvaceous body. He became instantly hard, filled with the memory of how it felt to have her in his arms, for the most explosive sexual night of his life. *He wanted her.* Here in Rio, beneath the Brazilian sunshine, suddenly he could think of nothing but taking her, right here and now. He licked his lips and said hoarsely, "But I didn't expect it to look like *that*."

An embarrassed blush rose to her cheeks as she pushed up her black-framed glasses in a self-conscious gesture. "I gained a little weight with my pregnancy," she mumbled. "I'm not so thin as I used to be."

"No." Gabriel stared at her, feeling his body tighten with lust. "No, you're not."

Willing himself to stay in control, he pulled out a chair at the table next to the pool. "Maria made breakfast. Come and eat."

Laura scowled. "Is that an order?"

"Sim."

Carefully folding her towel and setting it on a nearby table—instead of just dropping it to the floor, as he would have done—she sat down.

"I probably shouldn't eat anything. Not if I'm supposed to wear a bikini," she said in a low voice. "I've tried to diet, but…"

"Never diet again," he said tersely. "You are perfect."

He pushed her chair back under the table. He paused, allowing his hands to remain on the back of the chair, next to her shoulders. He could almost feel the warmth of her soft skin.

She looked up at him over her shoulder with a scowl. "You're just being nice."

He stared down at her. "When have you ever known me to be nice?"

Her full pink lips suddenly curved into a smile as her blue eyes twinkled. "Good point." She tilted her head, considering. "So you really think I look…all right?"

"Hmm." His eyes lingered on her spectacular figure. She'd been beautiful before, but now, it was almost like torture to see her perfect female shape. Those hips. Her curvaceous bottom. Those breasts—!

She was almost *too* attractive, he thought. He wanted to convince Oliveira and Adriana he was in love with Laura, not have every other man on the Avenida Vieira Souta enjoy the luscious spectacle of her body. "You're fine," he said, irritated. "But that dress is unacceptable. We'll buy you something else when we go shopping today."

"Shopping. Right." Pouring milk and sugar into her cup, she stirred her coffee with a silver spoon. "I can hardly wait."

He sat down across the table. "You have nothing to worry about." He pushed the bread basket toward her. "It'll be fine."

She took a roll and sipped her coffee, and as they ate, Gabriel couldn't stop staring at her. Once, their relationship had been easy. A friendship. A trust. Now, he couldn't quite read her.

Strange.

For five years, Laura Parker had been the perfect employee. She'd had no life or interests of her own. She'd always been ready and waiting to offer her competent assistance for his latest emergency, whether it was a billion-dollar drop on a foreign stock exchange or a broken thread on his tuxedo.

Now…there was something different about her. Something had changed in her over the last year. He felt as if he didn't know her.

"How is your meal?" he said gruffly.

"Delicious."

"Try this." He handed her a bowl of pastries. Their fingers brushed and she jerked away as if he'd burned her.

He scowled at her. "We're attending Oliveira's party in three hours. No one will believe we are a couple if you jump every time I touch you."

Putting down her fork with a clang, she looked at him. "You're right."

He held out his hand across the table, palm up.

With an intake of breath, she placed her hand in his. He felt her tremble. Felt the warmth of her skin. A rush of desire went through him as his fingers tightened over hers. Coming to her side of the table, he pulled her to her feet.

For a moment, they stood facing each other beneath the warm, bright sun. A soft sea breeze ruffled her damp hair. She wouldn't meet his eyes. Her gaze seemed fixated on his mouth.

She licked her lips, and he nearly groaned.

"I passed your test," she whispered. "I'm touching you without flinching."

"Holding my hand is not enough."

She visibly swallowed, looking up. "What—what else?"

He put his arms around her, pulling her close. He felt the softness of her body, felt her curves pressed against him as he rested his hands on her hips. Her tight black dress squeezed her breasts still higher in the force of his embrace, plump and firm and begging for his touch. He stroked her cheek, tilting back her head. "Now I need you to look at me," he said in a low voice, "as if you love me."

Beneath her glasses, her wide-set blue eyes glimmered in the sunlight, shining like the sea.

"And I," he continued roughly, "am utterly, completely and insanely in love with you."

She trembled. Then she fiercely shook her head.

"This isn't going to work. No one will believe you'd choose me over her."

"You're wrong," he said. "Adriana is beautiful, yes. But that's all she is. While you…"

Laura stiffened in his arms, lifting her chin.

He cupped her head with his hands. "You are more than just a pretty face." He stroked her bare neck. "More than just a luscious body." He rubbed his thumb against her full, sensitive lower lip. "You are smart. And too kindhearted for your own good. You sacrifice yourself to take care of others, even when you shouldn't." He pressed a finger against her lips to stop her protest. "And you have something else Adriana does not."

"What?"

He looked down at her. "You have me," he whispered.

Gabriel felt her hands tighten around him.

"Can you do it?" he asked in a low voice. "Can you pretend you're in love with me? Can you make everyone believe that all you've ever wanted is for me to hold you like this?"

Her face was pale as she looked at him, trembling like a flower in his arms. When she spoke, her voice was almost too quiet for him to hear above the noise of the music and street party below. "Yes."

"Then prove it." He felt her soft curves pressing against his body, felt how delicate and petite she was in his arms. Laura was so beautiful in every way. He felt the press of her full breasts against his chest. Felt the tendrils of her long damp hair brush against his hands as he gripped her back. He breathed in the scent of her, lavender and soap, wholesome and clean.

He was hard for her. Rock hard. And yet she seemed to think she was inferior to Adriana da Costa, who aside from her beauty was nothing but a shallow, spoiled brat.

Suddenly Gabriel knew he had to tell Laura the truth.

"I want you, Laura," he said in a low voice. "More than any woman. I've always wanted you."

She gasped, her eyes wide. "You…"

Then her expression grew dull as the light in her eyes abruptly faded. "You're practicing again."

"No." He cupped her face roughly. "This has nothing to do with our business deal. I want you. I've spent the last year wanting you. And now you're in my arms, I intend to have you."

He saw her eyes widen beneath her glasses, heard her harsh intake of breath.

"But for now," he murmured, "I will start with a kiss."

Then he lowered his head to hers.

He felt her soft, warm lips tremble against his own. For a single instant, her body stiffened in his arms. He felt her hands against his chest as she tried to push him away. He just wrapped his arms around her waist more firmly and held her tight, refusing to let go.

Kissing her was even better than Gabriel had imagined.

It was heaven.

It was hell.

With a shudder and a sigh she suddenly melted against him. He ruthlessly pushed her lips apart, teasing her with his tongue, plundering the warm heat of her mouth.

His kiss became harder, more demanding, their embrace tighter beneath the white heat of the sun. Slowly, she responded. Her hands stopped pushing against his chest, and moved up to his neck, pulling him down to her. When she finally kissed him back, with a hunger that matched his own, a low growl rose in the back of his throat.

He forgot their affair wasn't real. He forgot the deal entirely. He felt only his masculine, animal need to have her, the need he'd denied himself for too long. Lust swarmed in his blood, pounding through his brain, demanding he take total possession of Laura in his bed.

CHAPTER SIX

THIS *couldn't be happening.*

Gabriel couldn't be kissing her.

But the part of Laura's brain that was telling her to push away, push away now, was lost in the scorching fire of his embrace. As his lips moved against hers, mastering and guiding her, heat seared down her body like a hot jungle wind.

Pleasure whipped through her, pleasure she'd felt only once in her life before. But this was even better than her memory. As they stood on the penthouse terrace, she grasped his open shirt, clinging for dear life. She felt the warmth of his body, the hardness of his muscled chest beneath his cotton tank top. His strong thighs in khaki shorts brushed like tree trunks against her legs. He towered over her, making her feel womanly and petite as he folded himself around her.

The hot, hard feel of his lips seared hers, causing sparks to shoot down the length of her body. Her breasts felt suddenly heavy, her nipples taut. A fire of ache raced to her deepest core as tension coiled inside her. She felt the rough sandpaper of his chin against hers and breathed in his intoxicating scent of musk and spice. Her knees shook beneath her. Her world was spinning.

Everything she'd wanted, everything she'd dreamed about for the past lonely year, and five years before that, was suddenly in her grasp.

His hands stroked her back through her black dress.

"Come to bed with me," he whispered against her skin.

Bed.

She sucked in her breath as reason returned. He was seducing her. And so easily. She'd made the mistake of giving in to her desire for him once, and it had changed the course of her life. She couldn't let it happen again. Never again…

With a ragged gasp, she pulled away from his grasp. Breathing hard, she glared up at him. "You don't seriously expect me to fall into bed with you after one practice kiss?"

His half-lidded eyes were sultry with confidence—*arrogance*—and his sensual lips curved into a smile. "Yes. I had rather hoped you would."

"Forget it."

"It would make our pretend affair more believable."

"By turning it into a real one?" she whispered.

He shrugged, even as the intensity of his gaze belied that casual gesture. "Why not?"

The early afternoon was growing hot, the sun and humidity alleviated only by the cooling trade winds off the Atlantic and the Janeiro River, for which the city had been named. Laura took a deep breath of the fragrant, fresh air redolent of spices and tropical fruits. How many times had she prayed that by some miracle, Gabriel would come for her?

I want you, Laura, more than any woman. I've always wanted you.

She pushed aside her own longing. She couldn't let herself want him. She couldn't. She lifted her chin. "Thanks, but I'm not interested in a one-night stand."

His black eyes glowed like embers. "I don't want a one-night stand."

She licked her suddenly dry lips. "You—you don't?"

He shook his head. "I want you to stay."

"You do?"

"I've missed having you as my secretary. And," he added, as she folded her arms furiously, "as my lover."

"Oh." Her arms fell back to her sides. She whispered, "And Robby?"

His jaw hardened as he looked away.

"The two of you can live in the apartment below mine," he said. "Your child need not inconvenience me at all."

Your child. Hot pride and anger rushed back to her, stiffening her spine. "You mean you will kindly over-look my baby in order to have me in Rio as your 24/7 employee and late-night booty call."

He stared at her, wide-eyed. Then he gave a sudden laugh. "I've missed you, Laura," he said softly. "No one stands up to me like you do. You're not afraid of me at all. You see right through me. I like that."

She jerked away from him, near tears and furious with herself. She couldn't believe she'd let herself get seduced by his sweet kisses, not even for an instant. Absolutely nothing had changed. Gabriel didn't want a wife or child. And for her, only a real family would do.

"Sorry," she said coldly. "But my days of being your

work slave and casual late-night lover are *over*. Don't you dare kiss me again."

But his hands only tightened on her. "I can and I will."

She exhaled in fury. "You have some arrogance to think—"

Seizing her in his arms, he kissed her at once, roughly, hard enough to bruise. Showing mastery. Showing possession. And to her eternal shame, when his hot lips were against hers, she could not resist. She sagged in his arms—and kissed him back.

"I want you, Laura," he murmured against her skin when he finally pulled away. "And I will have you. If not this instant, then soon. Tonight."

She shoved her hands against his hard chest, his deliciously muscular, taut body beneath the tight cotton tank top… Maybe it hadn't been so much a shove as a caress. Angry at herself, she stepped back from him, her cheeks hot. With more confidence than she felt, she said, "Not going to happen."

"We'll see." His voice held a smug masculine tone.

"Our deal had nothing to do with sex."

"Correct."

"I don't have to sleep with you."

He had the temerity to give her a sensual, heavy-lidded glance. "And yet you will."

"Ooh!" Clenching her hands into fists, she gave a little stomp of her heel and went back into the penthouse. She found her son still playing on the spotless floor in the kitchen as Maria washed the dishes.

Gathering her baby in her arms, Laura took Robby into the living room and sat down in a new rocking chair by the wide windows overlooking the city. When Gabriel followed her, she glared at him, daring him to interrupt her time with her child. With a sardonic uplift of his brow, he just turned away, disappearing down the hall.

For long moments, Laura held her baby. She fed him, rocking him to sleep, and suddenly felt like crying.

She couldn't let Gabriel seduce her. She could *not*. No matter how much her body craved his touch. No matter how her heart yearned.

Because her heart yearned for a lie. Gabriel would never change. Getting close to him would only break her heart—again. Break her heart, and possibly risk custody of her son. If she fell into bed with Gabriel, if she gave him her body, she feared she would also give up the secret that had tormented her for over a year.

She looked down at the sweet six-month-old baby slumbering in her arms. Gently, she rose to her feet and carried him down the hall to her darkened bedroom and set him in his crib. She stared down at Robby for a moment, listening to his steady, even breathing. Then she stiffened when a shadow fell from the open doorway.

"Time to go," Gabriel said behind her.

Straightening her tight dress over her hips, she walked out of the bedroom and closed the door. She glared at him, then glanced behind her. "I hate to leave him."

"Your son will be fine. Maria will be looking after him. And anyway—" he lifted a dark eyebrow "—this one night's work will allow you to give him a comfortable life."

She took a deep breath. "You're right. A million dollars is worth it." She lifted her chin. "It's even worth spending a night with you."

His lips curved into a sensual smile. "The whole night."

"Not going to happen."

"We'll see." He turned without touching her, and after bidding farewell to Maria, they took the elevator downstairs. Carlos had the Ferrari waiting in the alley behind the building, engine running.

"Obrigado," Gabriel said to him in passing, then held open the door for Laura. "If you please."

She tottered into the low-slung Ferrari, feeling squeezed like a sausage by the tight black dress and half expecting to bust a seam. Gabriel climbed in beside her and the red sports car roared away from the curb.

As he drove through the crowded streets, Laura stared out in amazement through the window. Rio de Janeiro always lost its mind and found its wildest heart during *Carnaval*, and this year that was more true than ever. Music wafted through the air, horns and drums to accompany people singing. Impromptu parades marched through the streets, and even those not on carnival floats from the prestigious samba schools often wore costumes that sparkled with sequins—and barely covered enough to be decent. Everyone became sexier, more daring versions of their regular selves. Laura took a deep breath. Even her.

"I'm taking you to Zeytuna," Gabriel said as he drove. "From there we'll go directly to Oliveira's pool party."

"Zeytuna?" She'd heard of the large, exclusive boutique, but had never shopped there. She licked her lips and tried to joke, "They sell magic bikinis, right?"

As he changed gears in the Ferrari, he glanced at her from the corner of his eye. "Yes."

Yes. Just yes. No encouragement. No reassurance. Laura tried not to think of her looming bikini face-off with Adriana da Costa and the sheer humiliation that was sure to follow. She bit her lip and changed the subject. "So what is our story?"

"Story?"

"When did we fall in love? So I'll know when people ask."

He considered. "We had an affair last year," he said finally. "You quit your job and left me when I wouldn't commit."

"Believable."

He glanced at her. "But I missed you. I've been secretly pursuing you for months—video chats, flowers, sending you jewelry and love letters and so forth."

"Sounds nice," she said, looking away.

"You invited me to your sister's wedding, and we fell into each other's arms. You surrendered to my charm and agreed to be mine at last."

"A true Valentine's Day fantasy." Her lips twisted as she looked back at him. "And Robby?"

Gabriel blinked, then his hands tightened on the steering wheel as he stared at the road. "Ah, yes. Robby."

"Everyone knows you would never date a woman with a child."

"Yes." He set his jaw. Then, relaxing, he shrugged. "It will only add to the credibility of the story. It makes you unique. I wanted you so desperately, I was even willing to overlook your baby."

"*Overlook* Robby? Thank you," she said, folding

her arms as she glared out the window. "Thank you so much."

"I do not appreciate your sarcasm."

She looked at him. "I don't appreciate you saying you'll *overlook* my baby—like you're doing me some big favor!"

He set his jaw. "And I do not appreciate the fact that there is a baby living in my house."

"Because you must never be inconvenienced," she said mockingly. "The great Gabriel Santos must never have even a hint of family domesticity in his selfish bachelor's penthouse!"

Silence fell over the Ferrari.

"You love your son," Gabriel said. It sounded like a question.

Pushing up her glasses, she glared at him. "Of course I love him. What kind of question it that?"

Gabriel's black eyes burned through her. "So how could you allow yourself to get pregnant without also giving him a father? You always told me you wanted marriage, Laura. A home near your family. A career that would allow you time to raise your children. How could you toss all that aside for the sake of a one-night stand?"

She swallowed, blinking back tears. Yes, how could she?

His eyes turned back to the road. "You quit without notice last year," he said coldly. "*That* was inconvenient."

She stiffened. "Inconvenient to replace me in your office—or your bed?"

His lips tightened. "Both."

"So difficult, and yet you didn't bother to even try to talk me out of it."

They stopped at a red light. He turned on her, his eyes glinting with fury. "I let you go, Laura. For your own good, so you could have the life you wanted. But instead of following your dreams, you threw it all away. You made my sacrifice worthless. How could you? How could you be so careless?"

"It was an accident!"

"I told you." His eyes were hard. "There are no accidents. Only mistakes."

"And I told you, my baby is not a mistake!"

"Are you saying you got pregnant on purpose?"

Her mouth went dry.

He waited, then the light turned green. His lip twisted as he turned back to the road. "Every child deserves to be born into a stable home with two parents. I'm disappointed in you, Laura. You should have been careful."

Laura stiffened. "Careful like who? Like you?"

"Yes."

She longed to have the satisfaction of wiping that scornful, judgmental look off his face. She wondered what he would say if she told him that he was the father.

But she knew the satisfaction would be short-lived. If he knew Robby was his child, he might feel duty-bound to take responsibility for a child he couldn't love, and be pinned down to a domestic life he'd never wanted. And he would hate not just Laura for that, he'd hate Robby, as well.

She had to keep the secret. *Had to.* Leaning back against the black leather seat, she pressed her lips shut. *Just a few more hours*, she told herself desperately.

Tomorrow she and Robby would be on the plane back home, a million dollars richer.

"I thought family meant everything to you."

She opened her eyes, blinking back tears. "It does."

"I thought you were better than that."

"Don't you think I want a father for Robby? Don't you think I want to give him the same loving family I had?"

"So why didn't you?" Gabriel took a deep breath and said in a low voice, "Badly done, Laura."

She started to deliver a sharp retort; then stopped when she saw the stark expression on his face.

"Why are you like this?" she said. "Why do you care so much?"

"I don't," he said coldly.

"You do. You've always acted like you despise the idea of matrimony and commitment and children—all of it. But you don't," she said softly. "You care."

Gabriel pulled the Ferrari to an abrupt halt. He didn't look at her. "We're here."

Blinking in surprise, she saw they'd arrived at the enormous, exclusive Zeytuna boutique in the Leblon district. Her door opened, and she saw a young, smiling valet in a red jacket. Gabriel handed him keys, then held out his hand to her.

"Come," he said coldly. "We haven't much time."

Reluctantly, Laura placed her hand in his, and felt the same shock of sensation, the brush of his warm skin and strong grip of his fingers around hers.

"Are you cold?"

"No," she said.

"You're shivering."

She ripped her hand away. "I'm just afraid we will fail. That *I* will fail."

"You won't."

She looked down at her tight black dress, seeing her big hips and oversize breasts and a belly that was far from flat. She thought again of competing against Adriana da Costa in a bikini, and shuddered. "I don't see how."

Gabriel's sensual lips curved up into a smile. "Trust me."

He folded her hand over his bare forearm as if she were a medieval French princess and he was her honored chevalier. He looked down at her with eyes of love, and even as she told herself that he was only practicing, this time the shiver was not in her body, but her heart.

Pretending to love him was too easy. She was playing with fire.

Just a few hours more, she told herself desperately. Then she'd never see him again. Her family would never need to worry about replacing parts on the tractor or losing their home after a bad harvest. They'd never need to panic when a glut on the market suddenly lowered prices of wheat to nothing. Her family would be safe. Her baby would be safe.

Her baby.

Laura swallowed. This was the first time she'd left Robby with a babysitter since he was born. It felt strange to be away from him. Strange, and dangerous to feel this young and free, with Gabriel beside her. He smiled down at her, and for an instant she was lost in his eyes, so dark and deep against his tanned skin.

It would be so easy to love him when he treated her like this. Even after she went home, she knew she would always remember his low, husky voice saying, *"I want you, Laura, more than any woman. I've always wanted you."* She would feel the heat of his body against hers when he'd seized her on the terrace and kissed her. She had new memories to add to the time they'd first made love, when he'd pushed her back against his desk, sweeping everything aside in his reckless, savage need. When their sweaty, naked bodies had clung together, their limbs intertwined in explosive passion.

Now, Laura's legs trembled as Gabriel drew her toward the two tall brass doors held wide by doormen.

"Boa tarde, Senhor Santos," the first doorman said, beaming.

"Good to see you again, Mr. Santos," the second doorman said in accented English.

Once they were inside the foyer, Laura looked up in amazement at a center courtyard two stories high, with a dome of colored Tiffany glass on the ceiling. But if the glamorous architecture was straight out of the nineteenth century, the boutique's clothes were as cutting-edge as anything she'd find on Fifth Avenue.

A bevy of pretty shopgirls rushed to wait upon Gabriel. "Allow me to help you, *senhor*!"

"No, me!" a second one cried.

"Senhor, I have something wonderful to show you!"

Laura scowled. She could just imagine what the eager girls wanted to show Gabriel. Turning, she glared at him. "How often do you come here?"

He snorted, hiding a grin. "Once or twice a month."

"Lingerie for all your one-night stands?"

"Suits for work. I'm known to tip well."

Laura looked at the fawning shopgirls, who were all staring at him with undisguised glee. "I bet."

"Sorry, girls," he said. "We already have an appointment."

"Mr. Santos," an older woman said in English behind them. "Welcome." She stepped forward with assurance, her red suit a perfect match to her short, sleekly coiffed gray hair. "I am ready to be of assistance."

"This is Mrs. Tavares," Gabriel told Laura. His hand tightened around hers as he turned back to the other woman. "And this is the girl I told you about. Laura Parker."

"Certainly, sir." Mrs. Tavares came closer. Gabriel stepped back, and Laura found herself standing alone, bereft of his strength, beneath the older woman's scrutiny. She examined a long tendril of Laura's mousy brown hair, then nodded. "Very fine material to work with, sir."

"Dress her for the beach."

"Which beach?"

"A pool party at a luxurious mansion on the Costa do Sul. It will be attended by famous beauties and rich men. Make her shine above the rest."

Still staring at Laura, the older woman stroked her chin thoughtfully. "How obvious do you wish her beauty to be?"

"Completely," he said.

"It will require help from a salon."

"As you wish."

The woman pulled the black-rimmed glasses off Laura's face.

"Hey!" Laura protested.

"And an optometrist."

Gabriel smiled. "I leave her in your hands."

Laura's cheeks were hot. The perfectly coiffed, elegant woman continued to walk around her, looking her up and down in the tight black dress, as if she were a handyman and Laura were a sad, decrepit old house in need of a complete remodel.

"This isn't going to work," Laura said, fidgeting uncomfortably. "I think you should go to the pool party without me. I'll just go to the Fantasy Ball later."

"You go to the Fantasia tonight?" Mrs. Tavares gasped. "The *Baile de Gala*?"

"Yes, and she needs a ball gown," Gabriel said. "Casual clothes as well. But she must be ready for the party in two hours."

Mrs. Tavares froze. "So little time?"

"Desculpa."

The woman tilted her head, considering Laura. "It will not be cheap. Or easy."

"Cost does not matter. Just results. Satisfy my requirements and you'll be generously rewarded."

The older woman's expression didn't change, but Laura saw her sudden stillness. Looking at Gabriel, she gave a slow, respectful nod. "It will be done, *senhor*, as you wish."

"My driver will pick her up in two hours."

With a clap of her hands, Mrs. Tavares turned and started barking out orders to the young shopgirls in Portuguese. With a second clap of her hands she scattered them.

"Tchau," Gabriel said to Laura, kissing her on both cheeks before he turned away.

He was abandoning her to face the sharks alone? Laura gasped, "You can't leave!"

"Missing me already?"

"Hardly!" she retorted witheringly, even as she looked around her nervously.

"You're in good hands," Gabriel said. "Carlos will bring you to Oliveira's mansion. I have business to attend to, unfortunately. But I'll be waiting for you at the party."

"But what if…what if you're disappointed? What if my makeover is a failure? What if—"

Gabriel leaned forward to whisper in her ear, "Have fun."

Fun? Laura glared at him, her heart in her throat. What kind of fun would it be to look like a fool, to be nearly naked in front of Rio's notoriously body-conscious crowd, to be compared to Adriana da Costa in a bikini? She shook her head desperately and said for about the millionth time, "This isn't going to work!"

He gave her an annoyingly confident smile. "You're going to love this."

"You will not be disappointed, Mr. Santos," the older woman said, gently pulling Laura back into her clutches. Laura was suddenly aware that there were twenty sales-girls hovering around her, while all the other custom-ers were being chased out of this expensive, exclusive store.

The two-story luxury boutique had just closed—for her.

"No," she whispered, feeling scared that she would let Gabriel down. "You're wrong about me. I'll never be a beauty."

"You are the one who is wrong." Gabriel's eyebrows

lowered fiercely as he looked down at her, his dark black eyes glittering. "Today, the whole world will see how beautiful you really are."

CHAPTER SEVEN

OLIVEIRA'S party was in full swing when Gabriel arrived.

Security was tight for this event, one of the most coveted private parties of the *Carnaval* season. Not for tourists or international celebrities, this was for well-connected Cariocas, the richest local tycoons and their glamorous mistresses and wives.

Gabriel was grimly sure he'd gotten this invitation only so that Felipe Oliveira could taunt him in public that he'd decided to sell Açoazul SA to someone else.

And where was Laura? Gabriel cursed softly under his breath. He'd arrived ten minutes late, after an urgent phone call from London. He needed Laura here at once, so he could introduce her to Felipe Oliveira and try to undo the damage that Adriana had spitefully caused.

Oliveira's mansion was on the most beautiful stretch of the Costa do Sul to the north of Rio. The sprawling house was a white classical confection like a wedding cake, surrounded by multilevel terraces, with a large pool that overlooked a private beach. Oliveira had been a workaholic all his life, but now that he was in his mid-sixties, he'd apparently lost interest in business in favor of possessing—and pleasing—a woman half his age.

It was the only reason he'd finally offered to sell the company back to Gabriel after almost twenty years.

Gabriel stood on the upper terrace, looking down toward the pool where he instantly saw Oliveira, wearing baggy shorts and a button-down shirt. The man was deep in conversation with French tycoon Théo St. Raphaël, who was definitely not a local, and whose presence here could be for one reason only.

Gabriel ground his teeth. The Frenchman wore a sleek gray suit. He alone among all the guests was not even pretending to dress for a pool party. Gabriel's hands tightened on the railing. The aristocratic French bastard excelled at breaking companies up for parts. The two had tangled before, and Gabriel knew St. Raphaël would like nothing more than to steal Açoazul from under his nose. All the assets of his father's company would be scattered around the world, coldly dissected for St. Raphaël's profit.

Gabriel narrowed his eyes. He couldn't let that happen.

But where was Laura?

Scowling, he glanced at his watch. Carlos had texted that they were on the way. But Gabriel would have to start on his own. Grimly going down the stairs to the lower terrace, he started walking toward Oliveira and his French rival.

"Gabriel," he heard a woman's voice coo behind him. Setting his jaw, he turned with a scowl.

Adriana da Costa smiled up at him from a poolside cabana, where she was holding court in her tiny bikini. Five half-naked young men surrounded her, offering her food she would never eat in a million years. Gabriel saw one particularly hapless youngster trying to tempt her with a platter of bread and cheese. Bread and cheese?

Adriana's idea of a fattening meal was menthol cigarettes and a handful of raisins.

Lounging in her chair, she lazily stretched her skinny arm up over her wide-brimmed straw hat as she looked up at him. In her other hand, she was holding a glass of something that looked like water but was likely vodka on the rocks.

"What a lovely surprise," Adriana drawled. Her eyes raked over Gabriel's shorts and short-sleeved shirt, now open over his bare chest without the tank top. "I didn't know Felipe invited you." She smiled slyly. "I heard the two of you ran into some sort of...trouble."

Gabriel set his jaw. She knew perfectly well why he hadn't been able to close the deal. Since Gabriel had ended their short tumultuous affair, Adriana had been determined to get his attention, and now she had it. She clearly wanted to either have him back in her bed, or wreak her revenge.

How he despised her.

Curving his lips into a smile, he walked past the young men clustered around her and stood at the bottom of her lounge chair, near her perfectly pedicured feet. "Does Oliveira know you are keeping such company?"

"Oh, these?" She shrugged, indicating her admirers with a wave of her hand. "They are just my friends."

"You are an engaged woman. You should not have such friends."

"Go away, all of you," she told them in English. Pouting slightly, she sat back in her chair. "It is easy for you to say. You pushed me into an engagement that I never wanted."

"I would never push anyone into marriage."

"Dropping me like you did, what did you expect me

to do?" She sat up straight in her lounge chair, leaning forward to expose her cleavage to better advantage. "No man has ever left me before. You wouldn't return my calls. I fell into the arms of the first rich man who proposed to me!"

Gabriel set his jaw again. "And that is why you are trying to destroy my business deal with Oliveira?"

She shrugged gleefully. "I just told Felipe the truth—that we were once lovers."

"You implied more than that," he said. "You made him believe if I moved permanently to Rio, I would make it my mission to lure you into my bed."

Adriana looked up at him like a smug Persian cat, fluttering her long dark eyelashes. "Wouldn't you?"

He stared down at her, unable to believe her vanity. She'd been a pain in the ass as a mistress, possessive and jealous. But clearly, she still believed that he, like any man, must be lusting after her as a matter of course.

He was tempted to correct that impression, but if he did, she might do some real damage and lie to her fiancé, tell him that Gabriel had made a pass at her. Clenching his hands with the effort it took to hide his dislike, Gabriel forced himself to say pleasantly, "I will always treasure our time together, but that time is over. I am with another woman now. In a committed relationship."

"Committed? You?" Adriana stared at him, her eyes wide and shocked. It was very satisfying. For several seconds all he could hear was samba music from the live band. Seagulls flew overhead, their cries mingling with those of the guests and laughter of the Cariocas lying out in the sun. She licked her lips. "That's impossible," she said faintly. "You will never settle down."

"And yet I have."

"Who is the woman?" she demanded. "Do I know her?"

"My former secretary," he said. "Laura Parker."

Adriana sucked in her breath. "I knew it," she declared. Her eyes glittered. "I always knew there was something between you. Every time you ran to her in the middle of the night, every time you explained why she was the only woman who could possibly live in your flat, every time you swore your relationship was innocent, I knew you were *lying*!"

"I wasn't lying," he said. "At the time, she was just my employee."

"She was always more than that!"

"All right. We were friends," he said tersely. "But never more. Not until last year, when—"

"Spare me the details!" Adriana hissed.

A wide shadow suddenly fell between them from the front of the cabana, blocking the sun's reflection off the pool. "Is there a problem?"

Gabriel turned to see Felipe Oliveira standing behind him. His shapeless shirt covered his large belly, and his eyes were hard as bullets in his jowly face. He must have seen Gabriel come down the terrace steps and apparently make a beeline for Adriana. *Perfeito*, Gabriel thought, irritated.

"No problem." He glanced at Adriana, who'd folded her arms to look away in sulky silence. "I was just telling your future bride that her love for you has inspired me to make a similar commitment. My secretary and I have had an on-off affair for the last year, and I've asked her to move in with me."

Silence fell, until Adriana cried, "Move in with you?"

Oliveira stroked his double chin with shrewd watchfulness in his heavy-lidded gaze. "So you've decided to make a commitment to another woman. How romantic. How very…convenient."

The older man was no fool. Deliberately, Gabriel shrugged. "Laura is everything I've ever wanted."

Adriana muttered a blasphemous curse. "I always knew the little mouse was in love with you."

In love? Gabriel frowned. Adriana was mistaken. Laura couldn't love him. She was too smart for that. She knew his deep flaws far too well. Laura wouldn't give her heart to an undeserving man who would break it.

Or would she? He paused, remembering how she'd let herself conceive a child by a man who wouldn't marry her, a man she didn't even love.

Adriana said scornfully, "With her adoring, sickening gaze on you all the time, I knew it was just a matter of time." She gave him a hard look. "But your relationship won't last. Because we both know you care about only one thing."

Aware of Oliveira watching them, Gabriel stared down at her coolly. "And what is that?"

"Power. Glamour. Blatant sex appeal. And your secretary does not have it." Adriana tossed her head. "She's nothing but a drab little nobody who…"

She paused, tilting her head. Gabriel frowned, then he heard it, too—a low hum of male voices behind them, rolling across the pool and terraces like gathering thunder. Adriana leaned forward to look around the doorway of her cabana. Oliveira and Gabriel slowly turned.

A woman had just stepped out of the mansion, and

was coming down the stairs from the upper terrace toward the pool. She was wearing a tiny bikini, typical attire for Rio. Carioca women were among the sexiest in the world, and the women at this party were among the most beautiful in the city. One new beauty should have been nothing, and yet something about this particular woman caused every man who saw her to stop in his tracks.

Even the young men who'd hovered around Adriana suddenly were craning their necks to stare. A waiter who'd come to refill Adriana's drink accidentally poured vodka on her bare thigh, causing her to curse aloud as she rose to her feet. "Oh, you stupid—get away from me!"

But no one was looking at Adriana. Not anymore.

The beautiful new guest was petite and curvy, her hips swaying as she moved. Long honey-blonde hair hung in waves down her bare back. She had creamy skin, and beneath the triangles of her top, the largest, most perfect breasts any man could imagine.

Gabriel's jaw dropped as he recognized her, this woman coming around the pool toward the cabanas with such effortless grace. The woman who had brought Felipe Oliveira's exclusive, glamorous party to a standstill.

Laura.

Laura trembled as she walked in her high heels. She felt naked in her bikini, passing through the crowds of beautiful, glamorous people who one by one turned to gape at her. Her legs shook as she walked down the stairs toward the lower terrace, where cabanas overlooked the pool and private beach.

She walked past the musicians, past the buffet table, where a handsome, hawkish man in a gray suit stood staring at her. She stiffened as she walked passed him, her head held high though her cheeks burned. People's heads were turning sharply enough to cause whiplash. Men's eyes widened. Women's eyes narrowed. Laura's hand shook as she pushed her mirrored aviator sunglasses a little higher up her nose.

Wearing this tiny bikini was almost worse than wearing nothing at all. It had been crocheted of natural, wheat-colored yarn. She'd never gone out in public dressed in so little before. She had barely ever seen *herself* this naked, always averting her eyes from the mirror when she came out of the shower. Now, she could feel the hot sun of Rio burning against her skin.

Or maybe it was just the flush of heat caused by all the eyes roaming every inch of her, tracing the lines of her breasts, butt and legs.

Laura swallowed, wishing the earth would swallow her whole. She threw a glance of longing toward the Atlantic on the other side of the terrace gate. She had the sudden yen to throw herself in the water and start swimming for Africa.

But she forced herself to keep walking, looking for Gabriel to the right and left. She couldn't run away. He was paying her a million dollars, and she couldn't quit just because she was scared. She was on a job and she would earn her money. Every penny.

But she wished she knew what people were thinking. Were they staring because they thought she looked nice? Or because she looked so hideously bad? As soon as she was out of earshot, would they all dissolve into scornful laughter?

Mrs. Tavares had taken her into the center of a whirlwind at Zeytuna, barking orders in quick-fire Portuguese, and there had soon been five stylists surrounding her, doing her hair, hands, toenails. An on-call optometrist had come to fit her eyes for contact lens. Laura had tried on hundreds of potential outfits for the pool party, for the Fantasy Ball, casual clothes for later, even lingerie. Though she had protested at the lingerie, her every complaint had been ignored. Laura's mousy brown hair had been highlighted. The stylists had started to prepare a spray-on tan to darken her skin, until Mrs. Tavares had stopped them.

"No. Leave her pale. Her creamy beauty will stand out from the fake tans of all the rest."

Laura's makeup had been done to perfection, so lightly as to be barely visible, and yet somehow making her look…good.

Mrs. Tavares had ordered her to try on many bikinis before she'd finally been satisfied with this one. Laura couldn't tell the difference—they'd all just seemed to be tiny triangles of fabric, barely covering anything at all. But the Brazilian woman had chosen this one, crocheted of soft beige yarn. *"Perfeito,"* she'd said. "It shows you off to perfection, Miss Parker. You are soft, womanly, with those curves. You are *real*." Mrs. Tavares's thin lips had curved. "You will stand out."

It was true that Laura's breasts had always been somewhat on the generous side, and since she'd left New Hampshire to have a secretarial career in New York, she'd gone to a great deal of effort to hide them, to make sure it was her professional skills that attracted attention, not her body.

"You have the perfect figure," Mrs. Tavares had said

with satisfaction as they'd stared at the result of Laura's makeover in a full-length mirror. "A Marilyn Monroe for the modern age. The gold standard of femininity."

Laura didn't quite believe her. A lifetime of feeling plain and unfashionable, especially compared to the glamorous women of New York, had left it imprinted on her mind that she was the hardworking one. The smart one. Never in her whole life had she been the pretty one.

But of course Mrs. Tavares would give her compliments, Laura had told herself as Carlos drove her to the mansion. The woman had been hired to give Laura a makeover, so naturally she would try to make the best of things. Laura had taken her praise with a pound of salt.

But still, the older woman had almost managed to convince her. Laura had felt confident, even pretty, when she'd left the boutique. Now, beneath so many open stares, she felt shy.

And afraid. What if, after everything, she failed Gabriel? Would he refuse to pay her the million dollars he'd promised? Or worse, would he just shake his head and look at her with cool dark eyes and say in a low voice, "I'm disappointed in you, Laura. I thought you were better than this"?

It had taken more courage than she'd imagined even to get out of the Rolls-Royce. Carlos had held her door open for almost a full minute, conspicuously clearing his throat before Laura had gathered enough bravado to get out of the car and walk into the mansion with her shoulders thrown back. Now, beneath the eyes of so many glamorous people, she felt vulnerable. *Exposed.*

Where was Gabriel?

Laura's feet shook in her ridiculously high heels as she walked around the pool. She didn't dare meet anyone's eyes, for fear of the scorn or mockery she might see there. She kept walking, keeping her gaze over people's heads, looking for one man who would stand out above the rest. She ignored the low hum of voices around her. She held her hand above her forehead, shading her sunglasses, as she looked for him. Would he laugh when he saw her? Would he regret whatever madness had caused him to think, even for an instant, that she could convince the world she was the woman who'd finally vanquished his playboy heart?

The thought made her throat hurt. Her hand fell to her side. She swallowed, suddenly unable to take the strain of all those mocking eyes on her.

"Que beleza."

Hearing Gabriel's low, husky voice behind her, she whirled around. She saw him standing in the doorway of a large poolside cabana. He was wearing shorts and an open shirt that revealed his muscular chest, tanned and laced with dark hair. Beside him she recognized Felipe Oliveira, looking sweaty and suspicious. But she was so relieved to find Gabriel that she hurried forward, pushing her sunglasses up on her head with a relieved smile. "Oh, Gabriel. I'm so glad to find you. I—"

Then she saw the woman standing behind them in the cabana and drew back with an intake of breath. "Oh. Miss da Costa. Hello."

The supermodel folded her arms icily. "I think we're a little past the politeness of 'Miss da Costa,' don't you? You must call me Adriana now," she said, in the exact same tone one might say *Go to hell.*

Laura blinked beneath the woman's malevolent

gaze. Then she remembered Gabriel's words. *You have something Adriana does not. You have me.* Looking at Adriana's angry expression, Laura realized their plan was working. The supermodel clearly believed Laura was Gabriel's lover—and hated her for it!

Straightening her shoulders, she looked at Gabriel with a smile. "Sorry I'm late."

He kissed her cheek tenderly. "I waited thirty-eight years to find you, *querida*," he breathed. "What are a few minutes more?"

He put his arm around her. After smiling at each other, they both turned to see the effect.

Felipe Oliveira looked skeptical. Adriana was scowling, sticking out her lower lip.

"You can't really be moving in together!" she said.

Laura glanced at him. Moving in together?

"It's already done," Gabriel said. He looked down at Laura, and his dark eyes were hungry and tender as he stroked her cheek.

Adriana gave a forced laugh. "She's no one. Nothing."

Gabriel wrapped his arms around Laura's bare waist. She nearly gasped at the rough feel of his hands against her naked skin.

"I am the one who is nothing." His black eyes burned through Laura's soul. "Nothing without you."

It's an act, she told herself as her heart turned over in her chest.

"All this time, you were right in front of me," he murmured as his wide, rough hand traced softly down her cheek. "The woman of my dreams." He cupped her face, tilting up her chin as he suddenly smiled. "I would fight them all for you."

"Fight who?" she whispered.

Staring at her, Gabriel gave a sudden laugh. Turning, he silently pointed behind them.

Following his gaze, Laura saw all the gorgeous party guests whispering to each other around the pool, staring back at them.

Of course they would stare at Gabriel, Laura thought. He was the sexiest, most sought after bachelor on earth. But they weren't looking just at him. Even Laura, inexperienced as she was, could see that.

And she suddenly knew, down to her bones, that they weren't staring at her because she was *ugly*.

She suddenly blinked back tears. Her makeover had created the illusion that Laura was worthy to be Gabriel's mistress. For the first time in her life, she felt beautiful. It was dizzying. Electrifying.

But the feeling hadn't been caused by magic fairy dust. She looked up at him.

It was the magic of his dark, hungry gaze. The magic echo of his words.

All this time, you were right in front of me. The woman of my dreams.

She was dimly aware of Adriana's angry scowl. But Laura didn't care about her anymore. Everyone else around them faded into a blur.

She and Gabriel were the only two people on earth. His dark eyes met hers, and his gaze fell to her lips. With agonizing slowness, he started to move his head toward hers. She realized he was going to kiss her, and her heart pounded frantically in her throat.

"Am I to understand," Felipe Oliveira said in a gruff voice behind them, "that this girl, your supposed lover, used to be your employee?"

Straightening, Gabriel turned to him, and Laura was able to breathe again. She leaned her cheek against his chest, still dizzy from how close she'd come to being kissed.

"His employee?" Adriana sneered. "She was his *secretary*."

Gabriel gave her a cool smile before turning his focus back on his rival. "Laura was once my secretary, *sim*, for five years. But now she's so much more." Looking down as she nestled in his arms, he stroked her cheek and said softly, "Now…she's the woman who tamed me."

CHAPTER EIGHT

IT'S only an act. Only an act!

But in spite of the constant repetition of those words, Laura's heart still didn't believe it as she looked up into Gabriel's dark eyes.

"Really," the other man drawled in accented English. His eyes traced over Laura. "She's certainly beautiful. But this is all too convenient." He folded his arms over his belly. "You've fabricated this affair, so I'll still sell you Açoazul."

Laura's pulse hammered in her chest. Convinced that their plan had failed before it had half started, she pulled away from Gabriel. But he held her tight in his powerful arms, even as he never looked away from the other man.

"Why would I do that?" Gabriel said coolly.

The man looked at Adriana's tall beauty, then back at Gabriel with a scowl. "You know why."

"You'd be a fool not to sell me Açoazul," Gabriel said sharply. "No other competitor has offered you a fraction of the price. Théo St. Raphaël certainly won't. Don't lose a fortune based on some unfounded fear!"

The older man stiffened. "I'm not *afraid*. And it's not unfounded."

Gabriel nuzzled her neck. "I'm not interested in any woman except Laura."

She leaned back against him, closing her eyes. The feel of his lips and the nibble of his sharp teeth against the sensitive flesh caused sparks to thrill down her body. She heard the other man hiss through his teeth, and opened her eyes. Felipe Oliveira and Adriana were staring at them with shock. Looking up at Gabriel, Laura shivered as a single bead of sweat trickled down her bare skin between her breasts. The air between them suddenly crackled with sexual energy.

"Come, *querida*," Gabriel said in a low voice. "It's getting hot. I need to cool off."

Wrapping her hand in his own, he pulled her away from the cabana and across the terrace through the open gate, past the security guards to the private beach. Turquoise waves pounded the white sand with a rhythmic roar. Laura glanced back at the party behind them. She and Gabriel were still in full view of the mansion and terraces as he led her across the sand.

"You did it," Gabriel said when they were out of earshot.

"Did I?" Looking up, she furrowed her brow. "He didn't seem to believe us."

"Of course he's suspicious. The man's not stupid. But we'll soon convince him we're in love."

"How?" she whispered.

He reached down and stroked a tendril of hair from her face.

"To think all this time I had such a beauty working for me," he breathed, then shook his head with a laugh. "I'm glad you didn't look like this when you were my secretary. I wouldn't have gotten any work done."

"You wouldn't?"

"It was hard enough as it was. You were always too pretty. I wanted you from the first day I met you, when you came up to my office wearing that old brown suit and big glasses."

He remembered the clothes she'd worn the day they met? "You don't have to talk like this." Her heart was hammering in her throat. "No one can hear us."

"That's why I'm saying it," he said. "Come on."

He yanked off his flip-flops and shirt, leaving them on the sand as he pulled her into the sea. Kicking off her high-heeled shoes, she followed him, almost willing to follow him into the very depths of the ocean as long as he kept hold of her hand.

He led her into the water, deeper and deeper still. She looked at him in front of her, and her eyes hungrily traced the hard curves of his muscular back, his strong legs. She felt the shock of cool water against her skin as they walked through the ocean waves, moving slower and slower until the water reached their thighs.

He glanced behind her. "They're still watching." He smiled. "You make this too easy. Any man would want you. Half the men here are in love with you already."

Laura swallowed, yearning to tell him she didn't care, that he was the only man she wanted, the only one she'd ever wanted. She'd once loved him with all her heart, this man with the warm dark eyes that made her melt, who whispered words of adoration, who made her body sizzle even when they weren't out in the hot sun.

Gabriel's sensual mouth curved. "And you've proved yourself every bit the skilled actress I hoped you'd be. The way you shivered and leaned back against me when

I kissed your neck, as if you were head over heels in love with me…they bought it all."

Except it hadn't been an act. Beneath the blazing sun, they stared at each other, thigh-deep in the cool turquoise water, swaying in the currents. She felt the splash of the cool waves against her hot, bare thighs.

He came closer to her. "The way you look at me sometimes…" His gaze searched hers. "It reminds me of something that Adriana said. As if you really…"

"Really what?" Laura whispered.

He pulled back, his self-mocking mask back in place on his darkly handsome face. "I think I really do need to cool off," he said with a laugh, and he fell back with a splash into the water.

When he resurfaced, Gabriel sprang from the waves like a god of the sea, scattering sparkling droplets as he tossed his black hair back. Rivulets streamed down his tanned, hard-muscled chest. She couldn't look away. She wanted him to kiss her. She wanted him to make love to her, hard and fast, slow and soft, and never stop. Most of all, she wanted him to love her.

He came toward her, his eyes dark. He took her in his arms, and she felt the hard muscles of his chest press against her bare skin. He looked down at her.

"I know what you're thinking," he said huskily. "I know what you need."

Her mouth went dry. "You—you do?"

Without warning, he lifted her up in his arms, against his wet, muscled chest. Her head fell back in surprise, and she had a brief image of the blue sea and distant green jungle before she realized what he meant to do. Holding her tightly in his arms, he fell back into the waves.

She had one instant to gasp in a breath before she felt the cool water splash against her skin and she was baptized by the waves.

When he lifted her back out of the sea, she sputtered in outrage, kicking her legs against his chest. "I can't believe you did that!"

"Why?" he said lazily. "Didn't it cool you off?"

"That's not the point!"

"It felt good. Admit it."

"It felt great," she muttered. "But you spent a fortune to get me to look pretty, and now you've ruined it. They spent ages getting my hair just right—"

"I haven't ruined anything." His arms tightened over her bikini-clad body. She saw they'd gone farther from the shore. The water now reached his waist, and she could feel the slide of the waves moving sinuously and languorously against her backside and thighs. Her cheeks grew hot as she realized the crocheted yarn bikini, with all its tiny holes, was transparent when wet. "I'm done with this party," Gabriel growled, looking down at her. His hands tightened. "I'm taking you home."

At the rough sound of his voice, a shiver went through her. Tension coiled low in her belly as his dark gaze devoured her with ruthless hunger.

As he started wading back through the waves, clutching her against his chest, she felt their overheated skin pressed together beneath the hot sun.

Against her will, Laura's gaze fell to his mouth, to the cruel, sensual lips that had kissed her with such passion. He looked down at her, then stopped. For several seconds, he just stood in the water, staring down at her.

Releasing her from his hold, he let her go, let her slide slowly down his body against him. She felt how much he desired her, felt his hard body beneath the water. His eyes were like fire.

Cupping her chin in his hands, he lowered his head to hers.

As he kissed her, she felt the hard press of his satin-smooth lips, the sweet, tantalizing taste of his tongue, the salty taste of his rough skin. She surrendered in his arms in the swaying ocean, floating on waves. Drowning in him.

As Gabriel kissed her, standing in the ocean, he felt the warmth of her naked skin in the swaying, cool water. He tasted the wet heat of her mouth. Suddenly, he knew he had to have her. Now.

He heard catcalls behind them in Portuguese and realized he'd forgotten about the party. He'd forgotten about Oliveira and Adriana. At this moment, he didn't give a damn about them.

He kept kissing Laura, even when she tried to pull away. She resisted. Relented. Surrendered. Then, with a gasp, she did pull away.

The waves rolled against their skin, pushing their bodies together as they stared at each other. Her eyes seemed to glimmer. With tears? Gabriel frowned. "Are you crying?"

"Of course not!" she said, rubbing her eyes.

He reached out to tilt her chin upward, forcing her to meet his gaze. "You're a terrible liar."

She looked away. "Don't women usually weep when you kiss them?"

Her tone was light, even sardonic. He felt as if he was in some strange dream as he looked down at her. This beautiful woman was Laura, and yet not Laura. "They usually weep when I leave."

She flashed him a glance. "If they're your employees, they're probably weeping with joy."

His lips tugged up into a grin against his will. *Meu Deus*. Even now, she could make him laugh, when all he could think of was dragging her back home, ripping off her tiny bikini and pulling her naked body into his bed. All he wanted was to be alone with her, to feel her soft limbs caress him, to pull her back into a red-hot kiss so explosive it burned him from within.

He would have her. Tonight.

I always knew the little mouse was in love with you.

He angrily shook away the memory of Adriana's words. Laura didn't love him. She couldn't. She was too smart for that. It wasn't love that existed between them. It was sex. Just sex. He shuddered. It would be, as soon as humanly possible.

"I'm taking you home," he said. "To bed."

The bravado fell from her beautiful face. She looked up, and her expression suddenly looked vulnerable. Young. The reflective waves of the water lit up her pale body, exposing her full curves, illuminating her beautiful face, which now seemed to hold new secrets.

"No," she whispered. "Please. I'm not like you. Making love…it means something to me."

Looking down at her beauty, Gabriel felt no mercy in his heart. She wanted him, as he wanted her. Why hold back? Why hesitate from taking their pleasure? Laura should belong to him, as she always had. She should be his. His unselfish act of letting her go last year had been a mistake.

And she'd had another man's baby. Sudden possessiveness raced through his body like a storm. Thinking of another man touching Laura left him in a rage. He wanted to get the memory of the other man off her skin. To make her forget anyone else had ever touched her.

With iron self-control, he took her hand. He heard her soft intake of breath as she stared up at him, her lips deliciously parted. His gaze fell to her mouth, but kissing her wouldn't be nearly enough. He led her out of the water and back to the sand. Stepping into his shoes, he grabbed his shirt, wadding it up in one hand.

"Where are we going?"

He glanced back at her. She looked as dazed as he felt. Her cheeks were flushed with passion, her lips bruised. "Home. Let Adriana believe we had to rush back to my penthouse."

"For an emergency?"

"I told you." He gave her a sensual, heavy-lidded look. "To bed."

He saw her shiver under the hot sun. Blinking, she knelt to pick up her high-heeled shoes. "But it's just a game," she whispered, sounding as if she were talking to herself as much as him. "It's not real."

Yet Gabriel was no longer sure. She'd come to Rio as his pretend mistress. Now he wanted to make it true. Where did the fantasy end and reality begin?

As he led her past security and across the lower terrace, he heard the whispers of the crowd racing ahead of them, a murmur rising like a wave of music. Gabriel didn't bother to glance at Felipe Oliveira or Adriana as he passed them. He was too infuriated by all the men staring at Laura. She did look beautiful with her long wet hair slicked back and beads of seawater sparkling on her skin like diamonds. And—Gabriel flinched—the yarn of her bikini was translucent when wet. Something he'd appreciated when they were alone, but now...

He bared his teeth at the other men as he led her across the terrace, a male predator protecting his chosen female. He climbed the stairs two at a time and entered the mansion, dripping water across the marble floors. As he led her toward the front door, he held her hand tightly. It felt so right in his. *Too* right.

He grabbed two towels from a uniformed attendant. "Tell my driver we are ready to depart."

The man hurried away. Gabriel took Laura outside to wait in the warm sun, away from prying eyes. Kneeling before her, he skimmed one plush towel over her bare skin, over her legs, her arms, the plump fullness of her breasts. Rising to his feet, he licked his lips and realized he was breathing hard.

He saw her swallow. Felt her tremble.

"Gabriel," she whispered, her voice hoarse, "Please..."

The Rolls-Royce pulled in front of the mansion, and Carlos leaped out to open the door, looking dismayed at his boss's early departure. He'd probably been playing dice with the other servants, Gabriel thought, but at this moment, he didn't give a damn about any man's pleasure but his own.

"Get in the car," Gabriel ordered Laura, his voice sounding admirably civilized compared to the roaring animal he felt like inside. When she didn't move, he grabbed her arm and pulled her roughly into the backseat.

As the driver closed the door behind them, Laura ripped her arm from Gabriel's grasp. "You don't need to be so rude!"

"Rude?" he growled.

"Yes, rude!"

Gabriel could tell she was hurt and angry. She thought he was being cruel. She didn't know it was all he could do not to push her back against the leather seat, to lay her flat on her back and rip off the little triangles of bikini. That all he wanted to do was taste those luscious breasts, throw himself over her, fill her completely. He clenched his hands into fists, shuddering at the sensual images that overwhelmed him. He wanted her—now. And he almost didn't care who saw them.

As Carlos started the engine, Gabriel forced himself to release her. He could wait until they got home. He could wait…

He repeated the mantra again and again as the car drove through the city. His body ached from the effort it took not to seize her in his arms. The slow drive though crowded streets, with police diverting traffic around sections closed for early evening parades, seemed to take forever.

Gabriel glanced at Laura sideways. The towel had slipped from her hands and the air-conditioning in the limo was no match for the way his temperature climbed every time he looked at her. Especially when he saw what the cold air was doing to her nipples beneath the bikini.

Water was still trickling from her wet hair, running slowly down her bare skin, down the valley between her large breasts. He wanted to run the edge of his fingertip down that trickle of water. He wanted to lap it up with his tongue. He wanted her spread naked across his bed, his body over hers, as he lowered his head to taste her, thrusting inside her, so deep, so deep…

As if she felt his gaze, she turned. Judging by the expression on her face, she hadn't been having such sensual images of him—oh no. She wanted to skewer him with a knife.

But as their eyes locked, her expression slowly changed. The glare slid away and her face turned bewildered, almost scared. With a visible tremble, she pulled the thick white towel tightly over her naked skin and looked out the window.

With a dark smile, Gabriel turned away.

She knew.

She knew what waited for them at home.

Memories of their one night together had caused months of hot, unsatisfied dreams for him. Now that he finally had her in Rio, he wasn't going to let her go. Not until he was completely satiated. He was done being unselfish when it came to Laura.

The car pulled up behind their building, but she didn't wait for Carlos to open her door. She flung it open herself and dashed out, heading for the private entrance.

It gave her a head start.

A low growl rose from the back of Gabriel's throat as he flung open his own door and raced out in grim pursuit. As he came around the car in the street, heading toward the curb, a red sedan nearly hit him. The driver honked angrily, but Gabriel didn't even pause, just leaped recklessly over the hood. He ran into his building's private lobby, across the marble floor. Ignoring the greetings of the guards, he ran for the private elevator just in time to see the silver doors slide together in front of Laura's face. Their eyes met for a single instant, and he saw the small smile that curved her lips. Then she was gone.

Gabriel cursed under his breath. He pressed the elevator button impatiently, multiple times, then rushed inside as soon as the door opened. When he arrived at the penthouse, he followed her voice.

"So Robby had a good day?" he heard her say from the terrace.

"Yes, Senhora Laura," Maria replied. "He had a good lunch, good play and is now having his second nap."

Breathing hard, Gabriel saw them through the windows, out on the terrace. The older woman was sitting in a lounge chair, with a glass of lemonade and the baby monitor on the table beside her, placidly knitting in the warm Brazilian sunshine.

"Did he miss me?" Laura's voice trembled. "Did he cry for me?"

"No, Mrs. Laura," she said kindly. "He had a happy day. But of course he will be glad to see his mama. He should wake soon. Perhaps you would like to take him on a walk?"

"Yes, I would like that. Thank you, Maria."

Laura turned and headed back inside. Gabriel ducked into the corner as she opened the sliding glass doors. Still holding her towel over her body, she started down the hall toward her bedroom.

He moved fast, springing like a jaguar. He heard her gasp as he shoved her through the open doorway of his room, pushing her against the wall. The towel dropped from her hands as he closed the door behind him with a bang. Grasping her wrists, he held her against the wall.

Without a word, without asking permission, he kissed her.

He felt the heat of her skin, covered only by the tiny bikini as he crushed her against the wall with his bare chest. Releasing her wrists, he grabbed the back of her head with his hand. Holding her tight against him, he kissed her savagely, hard enough to bruise, ruthlessly taking his pleasure.

CHAPTER NINE

WITH a gasp, Laura pulled back her hand and slapped his face.

"How dare you!" she cried.

The sound of the slap echoed in the bedroom. He stared at her incredulously, his hand on his cheek. Then his eyes narrowed. "Why are you pretending it's not exactly what you want?"

Laura sucked in her breath, feeling overwhelmed by need for what she could not—*could not*—allow herself to have. "Even if I want you, Gabriel, I know you're no good for me. It nearly killed me last year after our night together when you kicked me out of your life—"

"Kicked you out of my life?" he demanded. "You're the one who left!"

"You didn't try to talk me out of it. You didn't even ask me to stay!"

"I was trying to do what was best for you," he said. "I knew you wanted a husband, children. You needed a boss who didn't demand your life and soul. You needed a man who could love you as I cannot. So I gave you up, when it was the last thing I wanted! And what did you do?" He glowered. "You let yourself get pregnant by some cold bastard who cannot even be bothered to pay child support or visit his son!"

Tears streamed down her face as she shook her head. "Why do you keep torturing me about my pregnancy?"

"Because it means I sacrificed you for nothing!"

"Sacrificed?" she cried.

He grabbed her shoulders. "Don't you know how much I've wanted you, all this time?" His eyes searched hers fiercely. "Do you know how I've dreamed of you? In my office. In my bed!" His fingers tightened painfully on her shoulders. "If I'd known you would settle for so little, I would never have let you go!"

Panting with anger, they stared at each other in the shadowy bedroom, the only sound the violent rasping of their breath. His eyes were dark and furious with denied desire. His gaze fell to her lips.

"Laura..." he whispered.

She jumped when she heard Robby suddenly crying on the other side of the wall. All the shouting and the banging must have woken him.

"I'm not that virgin secretary anymore," she murmured, "free to make whatever stupid choices I want. I'm a mother now. My baby comes first." Setting her jaw, she pulled away from Gabriel. Stopping at the door, she looked back at him. "I gave in to passion once before," she said quietly. "And it nearly killed me."

Leaving him, she went to her own bedroom and locked the door behind her before she gathered her crying baby in her arms. Robby's plaintive wail instantly stopped as she cuddled him close. She breathed in the sweet smell of his hair.

She heard a low knock on the door.

"Laura." Gabriel's voice was muffled.

"Go away."

"I want to talk to you."

"No."

Silence fell on the other side of the door and she thought he'd left. She sat down in the rocking chair and held Robby in the darkness of the shuttered bedroom. Then Robby started to squirm and complain. Clearly, his nap was over and he was ready to play.

Setting her baby down on the carpet, with a pillow beside him in case he suddenly forgot how to sit and toppled over, she looked through the shopping bags that Mrs. Tavares had sent and selected some dark jeans and a white tank top. Pulling them on over a new bra and panties, Laura lifted her son onto her hip and quietly unlocked her door. Holding her breath, she peeked out into the hallway.

Gabriel stood leaning against the wall, waiting for her in jeans and a black T-shirt. His eyes were dark, almost ominous.

"Planning to sneak out?"

She took a deep breath, then tossed her head defiantly. "I'm taking my son for a walk."

"You need to get ready for the gala."

"It will just have to wait."

He stared at her, then set his jaw. "Fine. Then I'll come with you."

"Come with me?" she repeated incredulously.

He moved toward her quick as a flash, scooping Robby from her arms.

"Hey!" she cried.

Gabriel looked down at the baby, who was staring up at him with a transfixed expression. A shadow of a smile passed over Gabriel's handsome face. Turning, he opened the front closet and pulled out a folded stroller, an expensive brand that she would never have purchased on her own. Still holding the baby with one powerful arm, Gabriel opened the stroller with his other, in one easy gesture.

Her jaw fell. "How did you know how to do that?"

He shrugged.

She tried again. "Have you ever been around a baby before?"

He looked away. "It's madness outside. You are my guests. I will keep you safe."

"To protect us from a festival on Ipanema Beach? We're just going for a walk!"

"Funny. So am I."

"You're being ridiculous."

Putting Robby into the stroller, he clicked the baby's seat belt, then without a word, pressed the elevator button. The doors opened and he pushed the stroller onto it. Looking at her, Gabriel waited.

Exhaling, she followed him onto the elevator. The doors closed, leaving the two of them with only a baby stroller between them.

"Why are you doing this?" she said through her teeth.

"For my own selfish reasons, no doubt," he said dryly. "That is why I do everything, is it not?"

"Yes, it is." She bit out the words, then looked at him. "Why? Is there a chance Felipe or Adriana might see us?"

"There is always a chance," he said. "It's not impossible."

The elevator doors opened, and she grabbed the

handle of the stroller and pushed it through the lobby. Gabriel held the door open for her and they were out on the street.

Since she'd last been outside, the *avenida* had become even more crowded, filled with people celebrating *Carnaval*. Music was blaring, tubas and drums, as people sang and danced in the street with their friends, some of them wearing extremely provocative costumes as they gulped down *caipirinhas*, the famous Brazilian cocktail of lime and distilled sugarcane.

Laura and Gabriel walked down the beach to a slightly quieter area and found an empty spot past a big yellow umbrella. She saw families splashing in the surf with their children, as nearby, groups of young people drank together beneath the sun as they waited for the nighttime party to really begin, the women wearing tiny thong bikinis, the men in skintight shorts.

Laura took Robby out of the stroller, and when she looked around, Gabriel was gone. She placed her baby in her lap and Robby reached to take a handful of sand in his fist. She saw Gabriel across the beach, talking to a *barraqueiro*. A moment later, he was walking back across the beach toward her. He held up a plastic shovel and pail.

"I thought Robby would like to play," he said gruffly.

"Thank you," she said, shocked at his thoughtfulness.

He smiled, and the warmth of his suddenly boyish face as he held out the pail and shovel to Robby nearly made her gasp. As the baby happily took the shovel, Gabriel stretched out beside them and showed him how to dig in the sand.

Laura stared at him in amazement.

First he'd known how to handle the stroller. Then he'd thought of buying toys for their baby. He claimed he disliked children, so why was he acting like this?

Robby responded to his father's tutelage by first trying to chew on the shovel, then to eat the sand. Gabriel laughed, and with infinite patience, again showed him how to dig. Soon he had the baby in his lap. Robby was very curious about sand and kept dumping it on them both, then laughing uproariously. Soon deep male laughter joined with the baby squeals, and for Laura it was the sound of joy. She looked at Gabriel's handsome face, watching him as he smiled down at the child he did not know was his, and her heart filled her throat.

How could he not realize that Robby was his son?

"He likes you," she whispered. "And you seem to know how to take care of a baby."

Gabriel's dark eyes met hers. Then his expression abruptly became cold. He handed Robby back to her, causing the baby to give a little whine of protest. "No, I really don't."

All around them, she was dimly aware of the noise of the street party, of half-naked Cariocas tanning themselves beneath the sun, of people laughing and singing and making music all around them.

It wasn't too late for her to tell Gabriel the truth. She could tell him now. *By the way, Gabriel, I never took any other man as my lover. You were so careful to use protection, but guess what? You're Robby's father.*

How would he take that news?

He wouldn't be glad. Even in her most fantastic dreams she knew that. He'd told her a million times, in every possible way, that he didn't want a wife or children. Even today, when he'd asked her to be his mistress for real, he'd said he'd be willing to "overlook" her child. That he'd allow her baby to live in the downstairs apartment so he wouldn't be forced to endure his presence.

And worse. If there was one thing Gabriel resented almost as much as the thought of having a family, it was someone lying to his face. If he found out that Laura had lied to him for over a year, he would never forgive her. He would take responsibility for the child they'd created—yes—and he'd try to get some kind of custody. But he would not love their son. And he would *hate* her.

Tomorrow, she repeated to herself desperately. They would go home to their little farmhouse in the great north woods, safe and sound. She'd never have to see Gabriel again.

But that reassurance was wearing thin. Every moment she spent with Gabriel, seeing him with their son, she found herself wishing she could believe the dream. Wishing he could love them.

The truth about Robby hovered on her lips. But the rational part of her brain stayed in control, keeping her from blurting it out. If she told him the truth, only bad things could happen. And she'd no longer be in control of Robby's future.

Gabriel glanced at his watch. The sun had started to lower in the sky over the green Dois Irmãos mountain rising sharply to the west. "We should go. Your stylist is waiting at the penthouse."

"Stylist?"

He rose to his feet. "For the gala."

He held out his hand, and Laura hesitated. A wistful

sigh came from her lips. The brief happiness of feeling like a family was over. "All right."

She allowed him to pull her to her feet. Tucking a yawning, messy, sand-covered Robby back into the stroller, she followed Gabriel across the beach toward home. By now the avenue was so crowded that Gabriel had to physically clear a path for the stroller.

When they safely reached the opposite side of the street, he looked at her. "I'm looking forward to seeing your dress tonight." He gave her a sensual smile. "And seeing it off you."

He was so sure of himself it infuriated her. But as his dark eyes caught hers, her feet tripped on the sidewalk. He caught the stroller, grabbing her arm. Then, leaning forward, he kissed her.

"Nothing will stop me from having you," he whispered in her ear. "Tonight."

With an intake of breath, she felt butterflies of longing and sharp bee stings of need all over her body. Tightening her hands on the handle, she pushed the stroller as fast as she could toward the building. She told herself that the sexy, tender, strong man she'd just seen on the beach, playing with their baby son, was a mirage. She couldn't let herself be fooled by his act. Gabriel was always ruthlessly charming when he wanted something. And right now, he wanted her.

Gabriel Santos always won by any means necessary. Both in business and his romantic conquests. But once he'd had what he wanted, once he'd possessed her in his bed, he would be done with her. He would no longer be willing to tolerate the fact that she had a child. He would toss her out, or drive her out. He would replace her.

She licked her lips as he caught up with her. "What's going to happen tonight?"

His sensual mouth curved. "You already know."

She looked at his face. There was a five o'clock shadow on the hard edges of his jaw, giving his handsome face a barbaric appearance. "Felipe Oliveira is no fool. He's suspicious. What if after tonight, he still doesn't believe that you love me?"

"He will."

"And if he doesn't?"

Gabriel's dark eyes glinted with amusement. "Then I have a plan."

CHAPTER TEN

THE Fantasia gala ball was the single most sought-after invitation of Rio de Janeiro's *Carnaval*. Laura had read about it in celebrity gossip magazines in the United States. The glamorous event, held in a colonial palace on the Costa Verde south of Rio, attracted beautiful, rich and notorious guests from all around the world. And tonight, Laura would be one of them. Tonight, she would be Gabriel Santos's beloved mistress.

His *pretend* mistress, she corrected herself fiercely.

The door of the black Rolls-Royce sedan opened, and she and Gabriel stepped out onto the red carpet that led inside the palace, which had once been owned by the Brazilian royal family.

Gabriel looked brutally dashing in his black tuxedo. Laura felt his hungry gaze on her as he took her arm. She tried to ignore it, tried to smile for the benefit of the paparazzi flashing cameras around them, but her body shook beneath the palpable force of his desire.

I want you, Laura. And I will have you.

Liveried doormen in wigs opened tall, wide doors. Gabriel and Laura went down a gilded hallway, then entered a ballroom that sparkled like an enormous jewel box. Standing at the top of the stairs, Laura looked up in awe at the huge chandeliers glittering like diamonds overhead. From a nearby alcove, a full orchestra played, the musicians dressed in clothes of the eighteenth century, except with sequins and body glitter.

The guests milling around them drinking champagne, laughing, were in gowns and tuxedos that were even more beautiful. More outlandish.

As they paused at the top of the stairs, Gabriel turned to her. "Are you ready?"

Laura held her breath, feeling like a princess in a fairy tale, or maybe Julia Roberts in *Pretty Woman,* with her strapless red sheath gown and long white opera gloves that went up past her elbows. "Yes."

When Gabriel had first seen her in this dress, he'd choked out a gasp. "You are without question," he'd said hoarsely, presenting her with two black velvet boxes, "the most beautiful woman I've ever seen."

Now, Laura looked at him, tightening her hand over his arm as he escorted her down the sweeping stairs. A thick diamond bracelet now hung over her gloved wrist. Diamond bangles hung from her ears set off by her highlighted hair tumbling in soft waves down her shoulders.

She'd never felt so beautiful—or so adored. This ball was truly a fantasy, she thought in wonder.

Silence fell around them as Gabriel, the dashing, powerful Brazilian tycoon, led her onto the empty dance floor. Laura hesitated beneath the gaze of so many people. Then, seeing them, the orchestra changed the tempo of the music, and it was irresistible.

Within twenty seconds, other couples had joined them. By the second song, the floor was packed with people. But Laura hardly noticed. As Gabriel held her, she felt hot and cold, delirious in a tangle of joy and fear and breathless need.

He swirled her around on the dance floor, in perfect time with the music. She felt his heat through the sleek tuxedo that barely contained the brutal strength of his body, and all she could think about was the night he'd made love to her, when he'd pressed her against his desk and ripped off her clothes, taking her virgin body and making it his own. He'd filled her with pleasure that night. Filled her with his child.

Now, his dark eyes caressed her as he moved. Leaning her back, he dipped her, his handsome face inches from hers. Pulling her back to her feet, he kissed her.

His lips moved against hers, soft and warm, whispering of love that was pure and true. Promising her everything she needed, everything she'd ever wanted.

Promising a lie.

With an intake of breath, she jerked away from him, tears in her eyes. "Why are you doing this to me?"

"Don't you know?" he said in a low voice. "Haven't I made it clear?"

"We had a deal," she whispered. "One night in Rio. One million dollars."

"Yes." He looked down at her. "And now I'm not going to let you go."

She stared up at him, frozen, even as other couples continued to swirl around them in a dark, sexy tango.

"I'm not going to let you seduce me, Gabriel," she said, her voice shaking. "I'm not."

He looked down at her, his eyes dark with desire. He didn't argue with her. He didn't have to.

With a gasp, she turned and ran, leaving him on the dance floor. Looking wildly for escape, she saw open

French doors that led outside to some sort of shadowy garden. She ran for them, only to smack into a wall.

Except it wasn't a wall. A man grasped her shoulders, setting her aright as he stared down at her. "Good evening, Miss Parker."

"Mr. Oliveira." She licked her lips. Dressed in a tuxedo that only served to accentuate his bulk, he was drinking a martini beside the bar. Behind him, she saw the gorgeously pouting Adriana in a skimpy silver cutout dress that clung like spackle over her breasts and backside, leaving everything else bare down to her strappy silver high heels.

"Lovers' spat?" Felipe Oliveira said mildly.

Gabriel appeared behind her. He put his hands possessively on Laura's shoulders. "Of course not."

Swallowing, Laura leaned back against Gabriel, feeling the hardness of his body against hers, and tried her best to look as if her heart wasn't breaking. She forced her lips into a smile. "I, um, just wanted a little fresh air."

Gabriel wrapped his arms around her more tightly, nestling her backside firmly against his thighs as he nuzzled her temple. "And I wanted to dance."

Oliveira looked at them, his eyes narrowed. "You're both liars."

Gabriel shook his head. "No—"

"I'll tell you what is really going on," the older man interrupted. "You think I am stupid enough to fall for this. But if I sign those papers tomorrow selling you the company, you know what will happen?"

"You'll make a fortune?" Gabriel drawled.

His hooded eyes hardened. "You will end this charade and be once again free to pursue what does not belong to you."

Gabriel snorted. "Why would I possibly be interested in your fiancée, Oliveira, when I have a woman like this?"

The other man looked at Laura, then shook his head. "Santos, you change lovers with the rise of each dawn. Miss Parker is beautiful, but you will never commit to her for long. There is nothing you can say to convince me otherwise." He finished the last of his martini. "I will sell to the Frenchman."

"You will lose money!"

"Some things, they are more important than money."

Gabriel exhaled. Laura felt his body tense behind her, tight and ready to snap. "St. Raphaël is a vulture," he growled. "He will break my father's company up for parts, fire the employees, scatter the pieces around the world. He will crush Açoazul beneath his heel!"

"That is not my problem. I will not give you any reason to remain in Rio." Oliveira's jowly face was grim as he started to turn away, holding out his arm for Adriana, who could barely contain the smug look on her beautiful face.

They'd lost.

Laura's heart leaped up to her throat, choking her.

They'd failed. *She* had failed.

"You're wrong about me, Oliveira," Gabriel said desperately. "I can commit. I've always been ready to commit. I was just waiting for the woman I could love forever."

Frowning, the older man and Adriana glanced back at them. They stopped. Their eyes went wide.

As if in slow motion, Laura turned to face Gabriel, who was standing behind her.

Except he was no longer standing. He'd fallen to his knee.

He'd pulled a black velvet box out of his tuxedo pocket.

Opening it, he held up a ten-carat diamond ring.

"Laura," he said quietly, "will you marry me?"

Laura's jaw dropped.

She looked from the ring to Gabriel kneeling in front of her. She looked back at the ring.

I was just waiting for the woman I could love forever.

He'd changed his mind about love and commitment? Did he want her in his bed so badly he was willing to marry her?

He smiled, and everything else fell away. She was lost in his dark eyes.

"What is this?" Oliveira demanded. "Some trick? Now she's your pretend fiancée?"

Gabriel just looked at Laura. "Say yes. Make this an engagement party."

And Laura exhaled.

All her wedding dreams came crashing down around her. This proposal had nothing to do with love, or even sex. It was entirely about business.

This was his plan B.

Tears rose in her eyes, tears she hoped would appear to be tears of joy. Unable to speak over the lump in her throat, she simply nodded.

Rising to his feet, Gabriel kissed her. Tenderly, he placed the diamond ring on her finger. It fit perfectly.

Laura stared down at it, sparkling on her hand like an iceberg. It was beautiful. And so hollow.

"Hmm," Oliveira said, watching them thoughtfully. "Maybe I was wrong about you, Santos."

"You said you'd never marry anyone!" Adriana sounded outraged.

Never looking away from Laura's face, Gabriel smiled. "Plans change."

"But people don't," she spit out. "Not this much. You would never marry a woman with a baby!"

Stiffening, Gabriel turned to her.

"She has a baby," Adriana said spitefully to Oliveira. "They were seen together on Ipanema Beach. He just brought Laura here this morning, after they'd been apart for a year. Why would he suddenly decide he's in love with a woman after being apart for over a year? It's a trick, Felipe," she declared. "It's a lie. He's not committed to her. He won't commit to anyone."

"I can explain, Oliveira," Gabriel said through his clenched jaw.

Felipe Oliveira's jowly face hardened as he slowly turned to face his younger rival. "No," he said. "I'm afraid you can't. I don't appreciate this elaborate theater you've performed. The deal is officially off."

The man turned away. Laura saw Gabriel's frustration, saw his vulnerability and the desperate expression on his face as he lost his father's company forever.

"Wait," Laura gasped.

Snorting a laugh, Felipe Oliveira glanced back at her with amusement. "What could you possibly have to say, little one?"

"Everything that Adriana said is true," she whispered. "I have a baby. And I hadn't seen Gabriel since I left

Rio over a year ago. But there's a reason why he came for me. A very good reason he'd want to marry me."

Folding his arms over his belly, Oliveira looked at her with a shake of the head. "I am dying to hear it."

Laura didn't glance at Gabriel. She couldn't, and still say what she had to say. Closing her eyes, she took a deep breath. Then she spoke the secret she'd kept for over a year.

"Gabriel is the father of my baby."

CHAPTER ELEVEN

TREMBLING, Laura folded her arms.

"Ah," Felipe Oliveira said, stroking his chin with satisfaction as he looked from her to Gabriel with canny eyes. "Now I understand."

"No!" Adriana gasped. "It can't be true!"

Laura's gaze rested anxiously on Gabriel. His dark eyes were deep as the night sky. She saw him take a deep breath. Then slowly, very slowly, he came toward her. Never looking away from her face, he took her in his arms. Biting her lip in apprehension, Laura waited for his jaw to clench with fury and resentment. Waited for him to say something biting and cruel.

Instead, he gently kissed her cheek, then turned to face Oliveira and Adriana.

"We weren't going to tell anyone yet. But yes, Robby is my son. I wanted to wait until after our wedding to make it public. It seemed more proper."

"Proper?" Adriana sneered. "When have you ever cared about *proper*?"

Gabriel stiffened, glaring at her. "I have always cared about doing what is right," he said in a low voice. "I would never leave my child without a father, without a name."

"And yet," Oliveira said, shifting his savvy gaze between them, "you allowed your fiancée to raise your baby alone, for all these months."

Gabriel set his jaw. "I—"

"He didn't know about Robby," Laura interrupted in a whisper. "I didn't tell him. It wasn't until he came to my sister's wedding that he first saw his son. I knew Gabriel didn't want a family—"

"So he always insisted," Adriana said resentfully.

Gabriel's dark eyes glowed with warmth and love as he looked down at Laura, who was shivering in her red strapless gown and opera gloves. "But Robby changed my mind." He wrapped his warm, tuxedo-clad arms more firmly around her. "From the moment I saw Laura with our son, I knew I couldn't part with them. We were meant to be a family."

Laura blinked back her tears, hardly able to breathe as she heard the words she'd always dreamed of.

She'd told him the truth about Robby, and he knew it. She could see it in his eyes. Robby was his son. And this was Laura's reward for being brave enough to tell the truth. He wasn't rejecting her. He wasn't rejecting their baby.

All this time she'd thought it would be so hard to tell him the truth, but it wasn't. It was easy.

Staring at them, Felipe Oliveira stroked his chin. "You might be a bastard, Santos, but you wouldn't desert your son. Or your son's mother." He looked from Laura to Gabriel with a sly smile. "And I see the passion between you. I have been a doddering old fool to feel threatened. The two of you are in love." He gave a sudden decisive nod. "*Está bom*. We will sign the preliminary contracts tomorrow. Be at my lawyers' office at nine."

Gabriel put his arm around Laura's waist, smiling at the other man. "Sure."

Adriana glared at Laura. "You got pregnant on purpose! You tricked Gabriel into marriage!"

As Laura stiffened, Oliveira grabbed the supermodel's arm grimly.

"There's only one person you should worry about getting tricked into marriage," he said, "and that's me. I look at them—" he nodded toward Laura and Gabriel "—and I see love. I look at you, Adriana, and I see... nothing."

She stared at him, her eyes wide.

Oliveira lifted a white bushy eyebrow. "Our engagement," he said mildly, "is over."

He marched off across the ballroom. Adriana's cheeks went red as an amused titter flowed through the nearby crowd.

"Fine," she shrieked after him. "But I'm keeping the ring!"

Oliveira didn't even turn around. Frustrated greed filled Adriana's eyes, and with an intake of breath, she started to push forward. "Felipe," she whined, "wait!"

When they were alone in the crowd, Gabriel looked down at Laura. She took a deep breath, waiting for the onslaught of questions she knew were coming. "Oh, Gabriel. I know we have so much to talk about—"

"Wait." He glanced at the people around them, amused celebutantes and movie actors in designer clothes, rich and beautiful and dressed in sparkling, sexy gowns. "Come with me."

Grabbing two flutes of champagne from the tray of a passing waiter, Gabriel pulled her through the glorious, gilded ballroom, filled with music and magic, and out a side door.

The private garden was dark and quiet. Laura looked up and saw black silhouettes of palm trees swaying against the purple sky. The night was tropical and warm, and on the wild southern coast so far from the lights of the city, she could see stars twinkling down on them.

Biting her lip, she faced him. "So…so you don't mind?"

"Mind?" Smiling, he handed her a glass of champagne. His dark head was frosted with silvery moonlight as he leaned forward to clink his crystal flute against hers. "You are the most incredible woman I've ever met," he whispered. "Brilliant. Beautiful."

She stared up at him with trembling lips as joy flooded her heart. "You're not angry?"

"Angry?" His brow furrowed. "Why would I be angry? Because you lied?"

She licked her dry lips. "Yes."

He shook his head. "No, *querida*." His expression was tender. "I've just gotten everything I ever dreamed of. Because of you."

He drank deeply from his champagne flute, and she followed suit, her eyes wet with tears of joy. She'd never imagined he would react this way, not in a million years. What had she ever done to deserve this miracle—that Gabriel would so easily accept their child as his own? That he would be glad to be a father after all?

"I'm so happy," she whispered. Smiling, she wiped tears from her eyes. "I never dreamed you would react like this."

He looked down at her with a frown. "*Querida*, are you crying?"

"I'm happy," she whispered.

"So am I, my beautiful girl." He stroked her cheek, his fingertips lightly caressing her flushed skin. "You sexy, incredible woman," he breathed in her ear, causing prickles to spread down her body. Cupping her face, he lowered his mouth to hers. "I will never forget this night."

When he kissed her, his lips were hot and smooth on hers. He seared her with the sizzle of his tongue against her lips, teasing her. She gripped his shoulders, instinctively pulling him closer.

They heard a sudden burst of laughter as other guests came into the garden. Grabbing her hand with a low growl, Gabriel pulled her deeper into the trees, into a shadowy corner. Above them, palm trees swayed in the violet-smudged night. The other voices continued to come closer, and he pushed her all the way back against the palace wall. She felt the hardness of his body, the roughness of the stone behind her.

Without a word, he slowly kissed her throat. She closed her eyes, tossing her head back with a silent gasp. She felt his teeth nibble her neck, felt his hands skimming from her bare shoulders down the length of her arms, over her long white gloves. He kissed her bare collarbone, his hands cupping her breasts below the sweetheart neckline of her strapless gown. Pressing her breasts together, he licked the cleavage just above the red velvet, and she sucked in her breath.

Samba music poured out of the palace as the doors to the garden continued to bang open and more guests discovered the garden. Voices grew louder, laughing and sultry, murmuring in Portuguese and French, as other lovers approached their corner. Gabriel pulled away from her. "Let's get out of here," he growled.

She blinked at him, dazed with desire. "Leave the ball already? It's barely midnight."

Jerking her back against his hard body, he leaned his forehead against hers and whispered, "If we don't leave, I will take you right here."

Drawing in a breath, she saw his absolute intent to make love to her right here in the dark garden, against the wall, with people on the other side of the foliage and samba music wafting through the warm air. She gave a single nod.

Gabriel instantly grabbed her hand and dragged her through the garden, back into the ballroom. He pulled her through the huge, crowded space, wading against the flow of new arrivals. Laura heard people shouting greetings to him in a variety of languages, but he didn't stop. He didn't even look at them. He just pulled her relentlessly up the wide, sweeping stairs to the front door, where he tersely summoned his driver.

As they waited, they stood at the end of the red carpet, not looking at each other. His hand gripped hers, crushing her fingers through her gloves. She heard the hoarseness of his breath. Or maybe it was her own. Her heartbeat was rapid. She felt dizzy.

"What's taking so long?" Gabriel muttered beneath his breath. She felt his barely restrained power, felt the grip of his hand as if only sheer will kept him from turning to her and ripping off her slinky red gown, pushing her against the wall and tasting her skin, in front of all the servants, the valets and flash of the paparazzi's cameras.

It took three minutes before the Rolls-Royce sedan

pulled up and Carlos leaped out. Laura stared at the man's crooked tie. She saw a smudge of lipstick.

"Finally," Gabriel growled, grabbing his door.

"Sorry about the delay, *senhor*," Carlos said, casting a regretful glance back at the palace. Laura followed his gaze and saw a housemaid looking down from the second-floor window. Laura was so filled with joy, she couldn't bear the thought of everyone not being happy tonight. Standing on her tiptoes, she whispered in Gabriel's ear, "Give him the night off."

"Why?" he snapped. "I don't want to drive. I want to be alone with you in the back—"

"He was enjoying his time here." She tilted her head toward the window. "Look."

Gabriel glanced behind them, then instantly faced his driver, who'd just come around the car. "Carlos, you're dismissed."

"Senhor?" the man gasped in horror.

"Enjoy your night," he said. "I trust you can get a ride home tonight?"

Delight flooded the older man's face. "Yes, sir."

"I have an early appointment tomorrow. Do not be late." After opening the door for Laura, Gabriel walked around the car and climbed into the driver's seat.

Smiling at Carlos's dumbfounded expression, Laura fastened her seat belt, and Gabriel pressed on the gas. They drove down the tree-lined lane with a spray of gravel, and the flash of cameras from additional paparazzi parked outside the gate.

"I know a shortcut," Gabriel said a moment later. Turning off the busy main road, he drove down the rocky coast, the luxury sedan bouncing hard over the rough road. Laura looked out her window. The landscape was hauntingly beautiful, filled with trees and thickets of jungle that wound along the sharp cliffs overlooking the moonlit Atlantic.

She looked back at the dark silhouette of Gabriel's brutally handsome face, his Roman nose and angular jaw. She saw the tight clench of his hand on the gearshift, saw the visible tension of his body beneath his tuxedo.

As a warm breeze blew tendrils of hair across her face, she was so filled with joy she thought she might die. Life was wonderful, incredible, magical. How had she never fully realized it before?

It was Gabriel. He was the dark angel who'd changed her life forever. Her heart was his. Forever.

She loved him.

"Don't look at me like that," he said in a low voice, glancing at her. "It's a two-hour drive back to the city."

She sucked in her breath. "Can't you drive any faster?" she begged.

With a curse, he suddenly steered the car off the road with a wide spray of gravel, taking a sharp turn past a thicket of trees that ended on a dark bluff overlooking the wide ocean. He slammed on the brake and turned off the engine. The headlights went black, and with a low growl he was upon her.

But the front of the sedan hadn't been made for this. The two luxurious leather seats were separated by a hard center console, and the steering wheel pressed against Gabriel's hip. He'd barely kissed her before he was jumping out with a low curse. Opening her door, he yanked her out. She had one glimpse of the moon-drenched ocean beneath the cliff, and then he pushed her into the backseat.

He kissed her, his lips hot and hard against her, and covered her body with his own. She felt his weight against hers in the tight confines of the backseat. His scent of musk and soap mingled with expensive leather, the forest, wild orchids and the salty sea. The notched satin collar of his black tuxedo jacket moved against the bare skin of her shoulders. He gripped her gloved hands, pulling them back over her head, against the car window.

He kissed down her throat, his hands cupping her breasts through the corset bodice of her red dress. But their feet still hung off the end of the seat. His legs were dangling out of the car. And though the seat was comfortable and wide, he had scant space to brace his arms around her. With a low growl, he moved away, so fast he hit his head against the ceiling. He gave a loud, spectacular curse. She saw the flash of his eyes in the moonlit night.

"It's still not enough," he growled. "Not nearly enough."

He kicked the door wide open behind them. Taking her hand, he roughly pulled her out of the car. Kissing her, he pushed her back against the hood.

Laura gasped as she felt the warmth of the hard metal beneath her. Gabriel moved over her, kissing her lips, kissing her bare neck. Overhead, she saw the twinkling stars of the night sky as he peeled off her long white opera gloves one at a time, tossing them to the soft earth. She felt the shock the warm air against her bare skin. Standing up straight, he looked down at her as he yanked off his tuxedo jacket and tie, and she realized that he did not intend to wait until they got back to Rio.

Right here. Right now.

Below the cliff, she heard the roar and crash of the ocean waves pounding the shore. She heard the sounds of night birds and the chatter of monkeys from the stretch of dark forest behind them. She saw the flash of Gabriel's dark eyes in the moonlight as he bent over her, reaching around her to unzip her dress. He slowly pulled it down the length of her body. She watched in shock as he dropped the expensive dress to the ground. She was now lying on the hood of his Rolls-Royce, naked except for a white strapless bra, silk panties, white garter belt and white thigh-high stockings.

He gasped as he softly stroked her naked belly. "So beautiful," he breathed.

Swallowing, she looked up at him. The bright moon illuminated his black hair as his hands stroked her skin. Reverently, he undid the front clasp of her bra, pulling it off her body and dropping it, too, to the ground. She felt his shudder of barely controlled desire as he cupped her naked breasts in his hands. "I've wanted you so long," he said hoarsely. "I thought I would die of it."

Moving down her body, he licked the valley between her breasts, then took her nipple in his wet, warm mouth. As his tongue ran over her taut peak like a caress of silk, she felt his hands slide down to her hips.

Her own hands moved of their own volition, beneath his white tuxedo shirt to feel the smooth warmth of his skin, to feel the hard muscles of his chest beneath the scattering of dark hair. She unbuttoned his shirt with trembling hands as he breathed against her ear, tasting the sensitive flesh of her earlobe. He kissed a trail down her neck, to her breasts, as his hands moved between her legs, along the top edge of her garter belt and thigh-high stockings.

His fingers stroked over her silken panties, and her breath stopped in her throat. He reached beneath the edge of the silk, and she felt him stroke her lightly, so lightly, across her wet core. Her hips strained toward him but he took his time, holding back, stroking her. He slowly pushed two thick fingers an inch inside her.

She arched her spine against the hood.

Pulling back with a growl, he ripped off his white shirt, popping the cuff links. With a low curse in Portuguese, he bent over her once more. His bare chest was rough and laced with dark hair, his skin so warm as his muscles slid against the softness of her breasts. She felt him between her knees, his thickly muscled hips rough against her spread thighs. He leaned above her, standing beside the car. She gripped his shoulders as he kissed her neck, nipping the sensitive corner of her throat. With agonizing slowness, he kissed down between her breasts to her flat belly, past her white garter belt to the sharp edge of her hip bone. He kissed the edge of her white silk panties. Then he stopped.

She felt his warm breath against her skin above her thigh-high stockings. His lips slowly moved over the silk, kissing down her legs. Pushing them farther apart, he took an exploratory lick of her inner right thigh. As she sucked in her breath, he switched to her left thigh. She trembled beneath him, her breath coming in increasingly ragged gasps as his lips moved slowly higher on each side. He held her hips firmly, relentlessly, not allowing her to move away.

Pushing the silk of her panties aside, he paused, and

she felt his warm breath against her slick, sensitive core. He lowered his head between her legs, and still did not touch her, except with the soft stroke of his breath.

"Please," she gasped, hardly knowing what she was asking for. She grabbed his head, twining her fingers in his hair. "I—"

With ruthless control, he slowly pushed her wide with both hands. Lowering his head even more, he tasted her with the hot, wet tip of his tongue.

Pleasure ripped through her. With a cry, Laura flung her arms wide, desperate to hold on to something, anything, to keep herself from flying headlong into the sky. Her right hand found the car's metal hood ornament.

Gabriel's tongue moved against her, licking her in little darting swirls. Spreading her wide, he lapped at her with the full width of his rough tongue. As she cried out, he drew back, using just the tip of his tongue again to swirl against her in progressively tighter circles, until she twisted and writhed with the sweet agony of her desire. It was building—exploding....

"Stop," she gasped. "No." She gripped his shoulders, frantically pulling him up toward her, and he lifted his head. Undoing the fly of his tuxedo trousers, he yanked them down with his boxers. They fell to his black Italian leather shoes as he sheathed himself in a condom he'd pulled from his pocket. Leaving on her garter belt and stockings, he grabbed Laura by the hips and pulled her down to the very edge of the car hood, where he stood. Ripping the fabric of her panties in a single brutal movement, he pushed inside her in a single thrust.

She felt impaled by the way he filled her completely, so wide and big and deep. He gave a hoarse gasp and gripped her backside, lifting her legs to wrap around his hips.

Holding her against the hood, he thrust again, this time even deeper. He pushed inside her, faster and harder, squeezing her breasts as her hips rose to meet him. She felt tension coil low in her belly and held her breath as the sweet tension built, soared and started to explode.

Throwing her arms back on the hood, she closed her eyes and surrendered completely to his control. His hands moved to grip her hips again, speeding the rhythm as he rode her, so deep and raw that the pleasure was almost pain. So deep. So deep. Her body was so tense and tight and breathless that she didn't know how much she could take.

Her eyes flew open and she saw his face above her in the night, his features shrouded by shadow as he thrust so deep inside her that her heart twisted in her chest. He gasped her name and she exploded, clutching his shoulders as she heard a scream she didn't even recognize as her own voice. A man's voice joined hers as he plunged deeper into her one last time, thrust with a hard, ragged shout that echoed across the dark forest and crashing sea, causing startled birds to fly from the trees and disappear into the night.

Afterward, he collapsed over her, clutching her to him. Their sticky, sweaty skin pressed together as they lay on the hood.

When Laura came to herself, she realized she was wearing nothing but ripped silken panties and thigh-high stockings, beneath the dark Brazilian sky, on a remote stretch of coastline where any passerby could see them. She'd totally lost her mind. And it had been so, so good.

But Gabriel had won. He'd seduced her, just as he'd said. He'd possessed her.

And not just her body, but her heart.

She pulled away, intending to find her red gown in the darkness, to try to cover herself.

But he pulled her back into his arms on the long warm hood. "Where are you going?"

"You got what you wanted," she said bitterly. "You won." She shivered in the warmth of his arms. She'd surrendered and now she knew exactly the power he had over her—the power he would always have. She felt suddenly afraid of how vulnerable she was. He had her heart in his hands. "Now it's done."

"Done?" He gave a low, sensual laugh, then his hands tightened on her as he murmured, "*Querida*, it's only beginning."

CHAPTER TWELVE

By the time they arrived back in Rio two hours later, one thought kept repeating in Gabriel's mind. One thought over and over.

"Here," he said to her, covering her shoulders with his tuxedo jacket as they entered the lobby of his building. She threw him a grateful glance. Her red designer gown now hung askew on her body, the zipper broken from when he'd ripped the dress off her earlier.

As they passed the security guards, Gabriel glanced at them out of the corner of his eye. His white shirt was rumpled, the cuffs hanging open, his tie crumpled in the pocket of his trousers. Laura was looking at him breathlessly, her eyes luminescent, her makeup hopelessly smudged and her lips full and bruised.

He saw the security guards nudge each other with a smirk, and he knew he and Laura had fooled no one. There could be no doubt what they had been doing.

Normally he wouldn't care if people knew he'd taken a woman as his lover. But this was different. This was Laura. And one thought kept going through his mind, no matter how he tried to avoid it.

He never wanted to let her go.

Gabriel exhaled. When he'd taken her on the hood

of the car, beneath the night sky and in full view of the dark moonlit sea, he'd thought he would die of pleasure. Touching her naked skin, thrusting inside her until she screamed, holding her tight, the two of them joined together as one…

He shuddered. After that, he should feel satisfied, at least for the night. He should be satiated.

But he wasn't. Now that he'd had one taste of her, he only wanted more. And more. *He never wanted to let her go.*

Silently, they took the private elevator upstairs to the penthouse. The doors slid open, and he followed Laura inside. They found Maria quietly reading a book by the light of the lamp in the main room, beside the wall of windows two stories high.

The housekeeper rose to her feet, smiling. "The baby is sleeping, Mr. Gabriel, Mrs. Laura…" And then the older woman got a good look at both of them. She coughed, closing her book with a thump. "I will wish you both good-night."

"Thank you, Maria," Gabriel said gravely, and his former nanny scurried out, the elevator doors closing behind her.

After she was gone, Laura turned to him, a frown furrowing her brow. "You don't think she guessed about us, do you? You don't think she could tell?"

"Absolutely," he said, then at her horrified expression, he added, "not. Absolutely not."

She sighed in relief. "I'm going to go check on Robby."

Laura turned and went down the hall. He watched her go, watched the curves of her back and graceful sway of her body in his oversize tuxedo jacket as she moved like music. She stepped into the bedroom and disappeared. *Gone.*

His feet moved without thought, and he was down the hall and suddenly behind her in the darkened bedroom. He watched as she crept up to the crib and stood silently, listening to her baby's snuffling breaths as he slept. Gabriel came closer.

In the dim light of the tiny blue night-light plugged into the far wall, he could just barely see the sleeping baby. Robby's chubby little fist was tossed back over his head. His plump cheeks moved as his mouth pursed, sucking in his sleep. Gabriel heard the soft, even breathing of the child in the darkness, and something turned over in his chest. He felt the sudden need to protect this little boy, to make sure he never came to any harm.

Just as he'd once felt about his family.

The thought caused a raw, choking ache in his throat. Without a word, he turned and left.

He stood in the hallway for long moments, shaking. But by the time Laura came out into the hall a few moments later, he'd gathered his thoughts. Come to some decisions.

She closed her bedroom door softly behind her, then looked at Gabriel in the darkened hallway. "I'm so sorry about Robby," she said in a low voice. "I never should have lied, Gabriel. I was just so…scared."

Clawing back his hair, he gave a sudden laugh. "To tell you the truth, I was almost scared myself for a moment." He looked at her. "But it was brilliant of you to say I was Robby's father. It saved the deal. That was a stroke of genius, Laura."

Her beautiful face suddenly looked pale. "What?"

"It was the perfect lie. But don't worry. If Adriana

spreads the rumor I'm his father—and she likely will—I will not deny it." He set his jaw. "Since your baby's real father can't be bothered to give him a name, somebody has to do it."

She bit her trembling lower lip. "Gabriel—you never thought…for one moment…that it might be true? That Robby might actually be your son?"

He snorted. "No, of course not. If Robby were really my child and you'd lied to me all this time…"

"Yes?"

He shrugged. "I've destroyed men for less." Reaching forward, he smiled and stroked her cheek, then lowered his head to playfully kiss her bare shoulder. "But I knew Robby couldn't really be mine. We used protection. And you wouldn't lie, not to me. Other than Maria, you are the only person I trust in all this world. You are…"

But then he leaned forward, frowning at her. "You are crying again." He tilted his head, trying to see her face. "Is it from happiness?"

She looked away sharply, wiping her eyes. "Yes. Happiness."

"Good," he said. "Now." He stroked her cheek. "We must celebrate winning the Açoazul deal tonight." He gave her a wicked smile. "I can think of one way—"

"No," she blurted out. "I just need to—I need to…be alone."

Turning abruptly, she ran down the hall. He heard the soft whir of the sliding doors as she fled out onto the terrace. When he followed her moments later, she'd dropped his tuxedo jacket from her body. Her strapless gown was barely hanging on her full breasts, askew with the broken zipper.

"What are you doing?" he asked. "What's wrong?"

"Just leave me alone," she said. Her voice was low, almost grief-stricken. "Go to bed. I'll see you in the morning."

Her red dress suddenly fell to the ground, but she didn't seem to notice or care. He licked his lips, unable to look away from her half-naked body in the white bra and torn panties and thigh-high stockings. "What are you doing?"

She looked away. "I'm going to take a swim."

He smiled. "Wonderful idea. I'll join you."

"No!" she cried vehemently.

He blinked at her, frowning. "Why?"

For long moments, she didn't answer. He could hear the noise and music of the street party below them. She finally said in a low, muffled voice, "I need some time alone." When he didn't move, she choked out, "Just go away, Gabriel. Please."

Looking away from the illuminated turquoise water of the pool, she stared out at the vast dark ocean beyond Ipanema Beach. He'd seen a glimmer of tears in her eyes. And there was *no way* they were tears of happiness.

But she wanted him to leave. She'd made that clear. Setting his jaw, he turned and left her on the terrace, opening the sliding glass doors with a whir and closing them behind him.

Once inside, he stopped, clawing his hair back with one hand. He couldn't let it end like this. Did she have so much regret that she'd allowed him to make love to her? He turned around, intending to go back and argue, to plead.

Instead, he froze.

He saw her on the moonlit terrace, sitting on a lounge chair, her face covered by her hands. Then she dropped her hands. Squaring her shoulders, she started to roll down her stockings.

He stared at her, transfixed. She pulled off her garter belt and tossed that, too, to the limestone floor.

Rising, she stood in the moonlight. Now wearing nothing but her bra and panties, she walked to the edge of the illuminated pool. Ripples of water reflected tiny shimmers of light that moved across her naked skin. Gabriel stared at her as he touched the window, unable to move or even breathe as she stood on the edge of the pool, looking down into the water.

Then in a graceful movement, she dived in. She stayed underwater for so long that he was suddenly afraid. Sliding open the doors, he ran out onto the terrace.

He saw her sitting on the bottom of the pool, her eyes closed. It seemed to take forever before she finally rose to the surface with a gasp, her hair sleek and sopping wet.

Laura was facing away from him, the moonlight frosting her bare shoulders in silver. Her thighs spread wide as her legs chopped the water, which moved around her in illuminated ripples of blue.

He choked back a groan. He was hard and aching for her. There was no way he was leaving her now. Walking to the edge, he said, "Laura."

She turned to face him with a gasp. Her eyes were luminous, a dark shade of blue, as she tried to cover her breasts, treading water with her feet. "What do you want?"

Sitting on a chair by the pool, he looked down at her. "I want you to tell me what you're thinking."

"I'm thinking I want to be alone!"

"Tell me," he threatened. "Or I'll kiss it out of you."

Her eyes widened. Then she turned away. "Just go away."

But in spite of her defiant words, he heard a sob in her voice that caused his belly to clench. Had he done that? Had he caused it? His jaw set. Pushing the chair away, he rose to his feet. He calmly kicked off his black leather shoes.

"What are you doing?" she said, alarmed.

He didn't answer. Fully dressed in his tuxedo shirt and trousers, he jumped into the pool.

He'd been on the swim team in school, and was a fast swimmer underwater. He rose to the surface directly beside her, pushing her back against the hard edge of the pool. She gasped as she felt his hands on her.

"Tell me," he said grimly.

"No."

"Now."

Her eyes became wide and tearful. "I can't."

Gabriel looked at her, and again he had that same strange feeling in his chest, like a twist in his heart. Holding himself suspended in the water, he gripped the edge of the pool with both hands around her, trapping her. She had nowhere to escape.

"You're going to tell me." He felt the warmth of her curvy body against the sopping wet shirt now clinging to his chest. "Whatever it is."

He heard her intake of breath. Then she lifted her chin.

"It wouldn't do any good," she whispered. "Not to you. Not to anyone."

He growled in frustration. Holding on to the edge of

the pool with one hand, he cupped her cheek with his other palm. "Remember," he said roughly, tilting her chin. "You left me no choice."

And he ruthlessly kissed her.

Her lips trembled beneath his, soft and warm and wet. He moved his mouth against hers in a seductive embrace, luring her without force, tempting her with their mutual hunger, with the insatiable need between them. Deepening the kiss, he softly stroked down her cheek, down her neck. His hand went below the surface of the water and he stroked the side of her body, her plump breast beneath her nearly invisible silk bra, her taut, slender waist, the full curve of her hip.

With a shudder of desire, he pulled back to look at her.

In the moving prisms of light from the pool, he could hear the music and noise of the street party on the *avenida*. But here on the terrace of his penthouse, in the moonlit night, he saw only her. They were connected in a way he didn't understand.

He never wanted to let her go.

Reaching beneath her, he lifted her out of the pool. She was warm in his arms and her weight was light, barely anything at all, as he set her down gently on the limestone. He climbed out beside her, his wet tuxedo trousers and white shirt clinging to his skin. Impatiently, he pulled off the shirt, then yanked off his trousers with awkward force as the fabric clung stubbornly to his legs, nearly tripping him.

Laura, still sitting on the terrace floor in her transparent bra and panties, choked out a giggle.

"Laugh at me, will you, *gringa*?" Gabriel growled. He threw his sodden trousers on the floor, and his socks swiftly followed. He lifted her into his arms, holding her tightly against his naked body.

The laughter faded from her eyes, replaced by something hot and dark. Looking at him in wonder, she reached up and stroked the rough bristles of his jawline.

Just the gentle touch of her small hand sent his senses reeling, spiraling out of control. He wanted to push her into a lounge chair—that one, there at his feet—and throw himself on top of her, grinding into her, filling her until they exploded.

But he'd already done that once, on the hood of his car. No. Now, he would take his time.

Now, he would do it right.

Water trailed behind them as he padded naked across the terrace and back inside. The expensive rugs were left sopping wet with every step.

He looked down at her, this beautiful, soft, loving woman who had her arms wrapped around his neck and looked up at him with a mixture of apprehension, desire and wonder. He went down the hall to the master bedroom and set her reverently on his large bed.

He saw her lying across his white comforter, nearly naked, and he shuddered with need. Lines of silvery moonlight from his half-closed blinds slatted across Laura's bare skin, emphasizing the shadows of her full breasts and hips, and his whole body shook with hunger.

He needed her. *Now.*

"I'm going to get everything wet," she whispered with a nervous laugh.

"Good," he said roughly.

Her eyes were looking everywhere but at his naked

body, everywhere but the hard, huge evidence of his desire. There was no hiding how much he wanted her. Let her see. Let her know. He put his hand on the valley of bare skin between her breasts, and exhaled.

He could see her nipples through her wet silk bra. Beneath her transparent, half-ripped panties, he could see the dark curls of hair between her legs. He reached to rip off her bra, then stopped himself.

Take it slow. Do it right.

With iron control, he gently undid her bra and peeled it off her wet skin before dropping it to the carpet. Her panties were next—easy to remove those, as they'd already been ripped and only a few threads still held them together.

Looking at her now, naked and spread across his bed, he took a breath, struggling to stay in check. He wanted to throw himself on top of her and push deep, deep, deep inside until he felt her shake with joy around him. Instead, he forced himself to climb up beside her on the bed. Turning her against his naked body, he reached for her cheek and gently kissed her, long and slow.

His hand skimmed her side, caressing her. He took his time, kissing her, relishing the sweet taste of her lips, the warm wet pleasures of her mouth. He heard a sigh come from the back of her throat as she wrapped her arm around him, pulling him closer.

He throbbed against her soft belly, thick and rock-hard. But he made no move to throw her back against the bed. Instead, he just kissed her as if he had all the time in the world, exploring her mouth, biting her lip, nibbling her neck and chin, sucking the tender flesh of her ear. It nearly killed him to wait, but he owed it to her to take his time...take it—

He suddenly gasped as he felt her hand wrap around his hard, thick shaft. He jerked in her hand as she slowly ran her fingertips down his length. Her thumb gently touched the tip, and it became wet beneath her touch as a tiny bead like a pearl escaped. He gasped out a groan.

"Querida," he said hoarsely. "Don't… I can't…"

In a sudden movement, she flipped him on his back, pushing him against the pillows. He felt her lips move down his throat to his chest. He was suddenly in her power, and he felt it as she kissed his body. When her head slipped down past his taut belly, he gripped the goosedown comforter with white-knuckled control. Then he felt her tongue brush his hot, throbbing skin, licking the bead of moisture at the tip.

He gave a rough gasp and nearly lost it right then. Grabbing her shoulders, he pulled her up with force and lifted her hips over his body. He was blind with need, ready to thrust inside her, to impale her. He only knew he had to take her or die.

"Wait," she panted. Wrenching away from his grasp, she opened a drawer beside the bed. He saw a condom in her hand and realized he'd forgotten all about it.

He'd forgotten about it. If Laura hadn't stopped him, he would have made love to a woman without a condom for the first time in his life. He exhaled as he broke out into a sweat.

"There," Laura whispered. Finally, she lowered her body over his, allowing him to impale her, inch by inch.

His eyes rolled back and he closed his eyes. Yes. *Yes.* He was losing his mind. The more time he spent with her, the more he lost. And it was worth it. So worth it.

Slowly, she moved against him, pulling him deeper

inside her. Her thighs were clamped around his hips as she increased her rhythm and speed, riding him. Opening his eyes, he looked up at her, watching the sway of her enormous breasts as she moved over him. Her face was luminous. Her eyes were closed in ecstasy as she bit her full, bruised lower lip. He heard the intake of her breath, and he never wanted to let her go.

Ever.

His heart clenched in his chest. He couldn't let himself feel that way. He couldn't let himself feel anything but lust. Pure, raw sex.

He had to teach Laura her place. Show them both the true nature of the passion between them.

With a violent movement, he rolled her over on her back, so he was on top of her. Her eyes widened as he roughly gripped her shoulders. Then with a grunt he thrust inside her, hard and deep.

He gasped as he felt her body around him, hot and tight and silken and deep. She cried out from the force of his possession, but he didn't stop. He only rode faster, filling her with each thrust, deeper and faster, ramming himself inside her. He heard her shocked intake of breath and then she, too, began to grip his shoulders, her fingernails sharp in her answering frenzy of desire.

But it wasn't enough. He wanted to take off his condom, to feel her from the inside with his naked skin—

No.

The answer was like a blow. It was the one thing he could not allow himself to do. Ever. He could not be that close. He could not risk her conceiving a child.

Furiously, he rode her harder—faster—desperate to feel her tight sheath completely around him, to lose himself utterly inside her. As he slammed into her, he felt her fingernails cutting into the skin of his back. The pain only increased his pleasure as he rode her harder and harder until beads of sweat covered his forehead. He wanted to leave her raw, until he was utterly spent, until they both collapsed into oblivion.

He heard her cry out, her voice rising in a slow crescendo of joy. Tension sizzled down his body, leaving every muscle taut, crying for release. With a violent thrust, he filled her deeply, then held her tight as she screamed his name. He felt her convulse around him and could hold back no longer. With a savage, violent thrust, he filled her. He felt her hot and wet all around him and poured himself inside her with a shout, as his vision went black.

CHAPTER THIRTEEN

LAURA woke up with a start to see the soft curl of a pink sunrise through the windows. She sat up in bed abruptly, the blanket falling from her naked chest. Had she heard her baby next door?

She listened, and heard nothing except Gabriel's even, steady breathing beside her in the shadowy bedroom. Then she heard Robby's voice again.

"Ma...ma...ma!"

Quietly Laura rose from the bed and pulled a robe off the bathroom door hook. Leaving Gabriel's room, she went down the hall to her own, where she found her baby son sitting up in his crib. Whispering soft words of love, Laura took him in her arms. Holding him tenderly, she fed him, rocking him in the rocking chair. The baby, now yawning with a full belly, swiftly fell back to sleep.

But Laura knew she would not.

Putting him back in his crib, she went to the ensuite bathroom, closing the door silently behind her. She turned on the shower and dropped the robe to the floor. As the steam enveloped her body, she climbed into the marble shower. She washed her hair and stared bleakly at the wall.

She'd been so happy last night.

She'd been so *stupid*.

Of course Gabriel had thought she was lying when she'd claimed he was Robby's father. It had seemed a useful fabrication. Just like his marriage proposal.

She glanced down at the enormous diamond ring still on her finger. Her other hand closed around it with a sob. It had all felt so real. She closed her eyes, leaning her head back in the hot water. When she'd realized he still didn't believe he was Robby's father, her heart had split in two. She'd fallen into the pool, sinking into the water, hoping to forget her pain the way she did at the pond back at her farm.

But it had been Gabriel's touch that had made her forget, the searing heat of his dark eyes as he'd carried her to bed. For a few hours, she'd managed to forget her heartbreak, forget that she was in love with a man who didn't want her or their child. She'd managed to forget she'd be leaving him in the morning, with a lie forever between them.

He'd taken her in his arms and kissed her, his lips so gentle and tender and true, and she'd forgotten everything but that she loved him.

His hands had stroked her naked skin as he'd kissed her, his body hard and hot against hers on the bed. She'd lost her mind. Then she'd taken things into her own hands. Literally. A half-hysterical laugh escaped her. She remembered the hard, silky smooth feel of him in her grasp. The taste of the single gleaming bead on the tip of his throbbing shaft. She remembered the rough way he'd reacted, pushing her down against the bed and savagely thrusting deep inside her until she exploded with pleasure, blinding sweetness tinged with bitter salt like tears.

She blinked back tears as she stared across the steamed-up shower. It was morning now. Her left hand closed over the ten-carat diamond sparkling beneath the running water. Their night in Rio was over. Time to give back the ring. Time to take back her heart.

As if she could.

She'd go back home to her family's farm. Back to her lonely bed. Only now it would be worse than before. Because now she knew she'd always love him. Now, she'd never be free.

Who is the father of your baby, Laura? Will you ever tell?

She turned off the water and dried her hair with a thick white towel. She put on the plush white robe and left her bedroom, closing the door softly behind her.

Going to the kitchen, she turned on a light and made coffee. As it brewed, she poured milk and sugar into a big mug, then filled it to the rim with the hot, bitter brew. Blowing on the steaming liquid, she stood for a moment, alone in the house of sleeping males.

This could have been her home. They could have been her family. If only she'd fallen in love with a man who actually loved them back, a man who wanted a wife and child.

Carrying her mug, she went outside to watch the sun rise over the Atlantic. It was the last morning she would ever spend with both Robby and his father under the same roof. The last day she'd ever see the man she would always love.

She felt the soft wind, the breeze off the sea, and looked down at the beach below. She looked down. The party had ended, leaving only litter rattling along the empty street.

"There you are."

She turned to find Gabriel behind her in drawstring pajama bottoms. Her eyes unwillingly lingered on his bare chest before she met his gaze. His dark eyes twinkled at her as he held up a steaming cup of coffee. "You made coffee. Thank you."

She took a sip from her mug, relishing the burn against her tongue. "Sure." She drew a deep breath and turned back to the view of the ocean. "It was the least I could do before I go."

"Go?" There was something odd in his voice.

She turned back to face him, startled. "In a few hours, you'll sign the papers to buy your father's company. And Robby and I will go home."

Gabriel's handsome face looked suddenly grim. Setting down his coffee, he put his hands on her shoulders and gazed down at her. "I don't want you to leave."

"We had our night. It's over." She swallowed back her own pain, tried to smile. "We both knew it wouldn't last."

"No."

Laura gave him a trembling smile. "It was always meant to be this way."

"No," he repeated roughly. "Stay."

"As what?"

"As…as my mistress."

She licked her lips, yearning to agree, yearning to say anything that would give her relief from this heartbreak. But she knew that staying here as Gabriel's mistress wouldn't end her pain. It would only prolong it.

"I can't," she whispered. "I would always be waiting for the day you'd tire of me, and move on to another."

He searched her gaze. "Can't you live in the moment? Just live for today?"

Blinking back tears, she shook her head.

"Why?" he demanded.

For an instant, she almost laughed. He looked like a spoiled child deprived of his favorite toy. Then she sobered. "I don't want to raise Robby that way. And because…"

"Because?"

She took a deep breath. Taking her heart in her hands, she looked up at him.

"Because I love you," she whispered.

His dark eyes widened. "You—love me," he repeated.

She nodded, a lump in her throat. "I left you last year because I knew you could never love me back. You've told me so many times you will never love anyone. Not a wife." She trembled, lifting her eyes to his. "Not a child."

He stared at her, and Laura waited, breathless with the hope that he might deny it, that he'd say his time with Robby had changed his mind.

"There's more to life than love, Laura," he said, pulling her into his arms. "There's friendship, and partnership, and passion. And I can't do without you, not anymore. I need you. Your truth. Your goodness. Your warmth." He gave her a humorless smile. "It warms even my cold heart."

She caught her breath, then rubbed her stinging eyes. "I'm sorry, but I can't do it, Gabriel. I can't," she choked out. "I can't just stay here, loving you, while you give me nothing in return but the knowledge that you'll someday leave—"

He gripped her shoulders. "Marry me."

Her eyes and mouth went wide. "What?"

"Marry me." He picked up her left hand, looking down at the diamond on her finger. His lips curved upward. "You already have the ring."

"But I thought your proposal was a lie!"

"It was."

She shook her head tearfully. "So why are you saying this? We're alone. You've already convinced Oliveira. You don't need to pretend, not anymore!"

"I'm not pretending." Bending his head, he kissed her hand, making her tremble with the sensation of his warm lips against her skin. He looked up. "I need you, Laura," he said huskily. "I don't want to lose you. Marry me. Now. Today."

She licked her lips, feeling like she were in a dream. "What about Robby?"

Setting his jaw, Gabriel straightened.

"Perhaps I can't love him. But I can give him my name. I can give you both the life you deserve. And I can be faithful to you, Laura. I swear it."

It was so close to everything she'd ever wanted. Gabriel would be her husband. He would be a father, at least in name, to their child. And if some part of her warned that this was a fool's bargain, to marry a man who could not love her, she still couldn't resist. Her heart overrode her reason and she succumbed to the temptation of her heart's deepest desire.

With a tearful sob, she flung her arms around him in her bulky white cotton robe, kissing him as the sun finally broke, vivid and golden, over the fresh blue Atlantic.

"Yes!" she cried with a sob. "Oh, yes!"

CHAPTER FOURTEEN

Two weeks later, Laura stared at herself blankly in the mirror.

An elegantly dressed bride in a long, white lace veil and satin sheath gown stared back at her. It still didn't feel right. She picked up her neatly bundled bouquet of white roses and looked back in the mirror.

It was the morning of her wedding. In less than an hour she would have everything she'd barely dared to dream of—she'd be Mrs. Gabriel Santos. Robby would have his father.

So where was the joy? She should have been ecstatic with bliss and hope. So why, looking at herself in this beautiful dress, standing in a suite of this beautiful rented mansion outside her village, did she feel so... empty?

Gabriel had wanted to marry her immediately, in Rio, but he'd quickly given in to Laura's begging when she'd asked to have their wedding in New Hampshire, so her family could attend.

"We can get married in New Hampshire, of course we can, if that's your wish," he'd told her. "But after the ceremony, we must live in Rio. Do you agree?"

She'd agreed. She'd been lost in romantic bliss, and

all she'd thought about was getting married to the man she loved, in a beautiful wedding surrounded by friends and family.

She hadn't bothered to think about what would happen afterward. Gabriel had already signed the preliminary contracts to acquire Açoazul SA, and he now planned to merge the company with Santos Enterprises and permanently move the headquarters from New York City to Rio de Janeiro.

Starting tomorrow, she and Robby would live far away from her family, far from the people who actually loved them. Laura would be the wife of a man who didn't love her, a man who would offer only financial support to the child he didn't know was his son. A child he could never love.

Now, Laura was dressed in an exquisite 1920s-style designer gown and her great-grandmother's old lace veil. In ten minutes, she would go downstairs to get married in this beautiful place. The Olmstead mansion was a lavish house of forty rooms built by a now-bankrupt hedge fund manager, currently rented out for weddings. It sat among acres of rolling hills with its own private lake, a winter wonderland. And after the elegant ceremony in the gray stone library filled with flowers, a reception would follow in the ballroom, a lavish sit-down dinner of steak, lobster and champagne.

Laura had fretted about having such a luxurious wedding, worrying she'd steal her little sister's thunder from two weeks ago. Gabriel had smiled and picked up the phone. Within minutes, he'd arranged to send Becky and her new husband to Tahiti on honeymoon, via his private jet. He'd created college funds for young Margaret and Hattie, to allow them to go to university.

For their mother, he'd completely paid off the mortgage on the farm, and even helped out Ruth's dearest friend, a neighboring woman with a sick child, by paying for medical care.

All of this, and he'd still deposited the agreed-upon million dollars into Laura's bank account.

"A deal's a deal," he'd told Laura when she'd thrown her arms around him with a sob of delight. "I will always take care of you. That means taking care of your family."

Laura bit her lip, furrowing her brow as she stared at herself in the mirror. She had everything she'd ever wanted. And yet…

"Your family," Gabriel had said. Not *our* family.

He didn't love her. He didn't love Robby. And he still didn't know the truth.

What difference does it make? she argued with herself. Her love for Gabriel could be enough for both of them. He would still provide for Robby financially, living in the same house, acting exactly like a father in so many ways. What difference did the truth make?

Except it made a huge difference. In fact, truth was everything. Because without truth, how could there be love?

Her troubled eyes looked back at her in the mirror.

But if she told Gabriel now that he really was Robby's father, if he knew she'd lied to him all this time, she might lose everything she had. He would never forgive her for the lie. He might—almost certainly *would*—call off the wedding. Why would he take her as his wife if he couldn't trust her? Then he might sue for custody of Robby, and take her baby away from her out of duty—or even a desire to punish her.

But her conscience stung her. Didn't Gabriel deserve to know the truth before he pledged himself to her for the rest of his life?

She heard a knock, and her mother's smiling face peeked around the door. "All ready, sweetling? Your sisters are waiting and eager to be bridesmaids."

Laura took a deep breath, clutching her bouquet in her cold, shaking hands. "Is it already time?"

"Just a few more minutes. The last guests are arriving now…" Then, as Laura turned to face her in her 1920s-style gown and her great-grandmother's long veil, Ruth gasped, and her eyes filled with tears. "Oh, Laura," she whispered. "You're beautiful."

Laura's lips trembled as she smiled. "You look amazing, too, Mom."

Her mother shook her head dismissively at the compliment, then came forward to embrace her, looking chic in pearls and a mother-of-the-bride suit of light cream silk. "I'm going to miss you and Robby so much when you're in Rio," she choked out. "You'll be living so far away."

Laura fought back tears. Though she adored the energy of Rio, the warmth of the people and the beauty of Brazil, the thought of moving permanently to the other side of the Equator, far from her family and home, caused wrenching pain in her heart. If her husband loved her, it might be endurable. But as it was… Choking back a sob, she squeezed her mother tight and tried to reassure her. "We'll be just a quick plane ride away."

"I know." Her mother pulled away with a smile, even as her eyes glistened with tears. "My consolation is that I know you're going to be happy. Really, truly happy." She paused. "Gabriel is Robby's father, isn't he?"

Laura sucked in her breath. "How did you know?"

Her mother's smile widened. "I've got eyes, haven't I? I see how you are together. How you've always been. He's crazy about you."

Apparently her mother didn't see as much as she thought. Blinking back tears, Laura swallowed and said over the lump in her throat, "We have some…problems."

Her mother laughed. "Of course you do. There were times I was ready to kill your father. But now—" her voice broke "—the problems we had seem small. I would give anything to have him here again, arguing with me." She paused. "I know love isn't simple or easy. But you'll do the right thing. You always do."

Laura swallowed yet again. "Not always."

Ruth smiled. "Your father used to call you Little Miss Trustworthy. Of all my children, you were the easiest to raise. And now, the hardest to let go." Her mother shook her head, wiping away her tears. "Look at me. Here I am, making a mess of myself after Gabriel bought me this expensive dress."

"You're calling him Gabriel," Laura said.

"Well, what else would I call my son-in-law?" She kissed her daughter on the cheek. "He's not your boss now. A husband is quite a different matter." With a little laugh, she turned to leave in a soft cloud of lavender perfume. "Husbands need to be reminded not to take themselves too seriously."

"Wait," Laura whispered.

Her mother stopped at the door. "Yes, sweetie?"

Laura clenched her hands. The bodice of her wedding gown suddenly felt inexplicably tight.

She was standing on a precipice and knew it. The

choice she made today would change the entire course of her life. And her son's life, as well.

You'll do the right thing. You always do.

"I need to see Gabriel," she choked out. "Will you send him up to me?"

Her mother frowned. "Right now? It's bad luck to see the bride. Can't it wait an hour?"

In an hour, they'd be married. Not trusting her voice, Laura shook her head. With a sigh, her mother closed the door. Five minutes later, Gabriel appeared.

"You wanted to see me, *querida*?" he said huskily.

A lump rose in Laura's throat as she looked at her handsome husband-to-be, at the brutal power of his body barely contained in the sophisticated tuxedo. She was suddenly reminded of the last time he'd been in a tuxedo, when he'd kissed her in the shadowy gardens at the Fantasia Ball, then made love to her on the hood of his car overlooking the dark, moonlit ocean...

She set her bouquet on the vanity. "I need to ask you something."

His lips curved as he came up to her, stroking her face. "What is it, *minha esposa*?"

His wife. She swallowed, looking up at him.

"Do you love me?" she whispered.

He stiffened. Staring down at her, his handsome eyes became expressionless and dark. She waited, her heart pounding.

"I thought we agreed," he finally said. "I care for you, Laura. I admire you and I always will. I lust for you and want you in my life."

Her heart fell to her white satin shoes.

"But you don't love me," she said softly.

He set his jaw. "I told you from the start. I can't love anyone. Not a wife. Not children."

"But we will have them…"

"No," he said. He came closer, putting his hands on her shoulders as he searched her gaze. "Is that why you sent for me before the ceremony, to ask if I might want children someday?"

She nodded tearfully.

He took a deep breath. "I'm sorry, Laura. I thought you understood. Though I can offer you marriage, nothing else has changed. I still cannot offer you love. Or more children."

She blinked, staring up at him in shock. "No more… no more children?"

He shook his head.

"But why?" she cried.

He dropped his hands from her shoulders.

"You should know, before you marry me, why I will not change my mind." His jaw clenched as he turned away from her. Outside the windows, rolling white fields were dotted with black, bare trees. "My parents and brother died when I was nineteen. Because of me."

"I know you've spent your whole life trying to regain what you lost," she said. "But it wasn't your fault they died!"

"I was driving the car that killed them." His black eyes were bleak. "My brother had just eloped with a waitress who'd had his baby while we were away at university. He'd been living with her for months, keeping it secret from our parents that he'd dropped out of school. I visited their flat in São Paulo, where they were living with their baby daughter, barely surviving on the wages he could make as a laborer. This from my brother—who should have been a doctor!"

Laura took a deep breath. "So that's how you know how to play with a baby," she whispered. "You'd spent time with your niece."

He gave her a smile that broke her heart. "Yes," he said in a low voice. "But when my brother decided to marry the woman, I was sure she was a gold digger. I dragged my parents to São Paulo to break up the wedding, and we convinced Guilherme to come back with us to Rio. I hated the thought of my brother giving up all his dreams, just because he'd accidentally gotten some woman pregnant."

"Right," Laura said over the lump in her throat. "A child doesn't matter to you. Not like a career."

His jaw clenched as he turned away. "It was raining that night," he said in a low voice. "I was driving the car so my parents could convince my brother to see reason." Gabriel gave a hard laugh. "But instead, Guilherme convinced *them* he needed to go back and marry Izadora. 'Turn the car around,' they told me. I looked into the rearview mirror to argue. I looked away from the road only for a second," he whispered. "Just a single second."

He stopped, his face grief-stricken.

Laura stared at him, feeling sick.

"I slammed on the brakes. I turned the wheel as hard as I could. But the tires kept sliding, right off the cliff. I heard my mother scream as the car rolled, then we hit the bottom. They all died instantly. But not me." He looked at her bleakly. "I was lucky."

"Oh, Gabriel," she whispered, coming close to him.

She tried to put her arms around him, to offer comfort. But his body was stiff. He pulled away.

"I was wrong about Izadora. At my brother's funeral she wouldn't even look at me. I offered to buy her a house, set up a trust fund for my niece, but she refused with angry words. I'd taken her husband from her, taken the father of her child, and she told me she hoped I would rot in hell."

Laura shuddered.

"She eventually married an American and moved to Miami. My niece is grown now." He took a deep breath, and she saw that his eyes were wet. "She's almost twenty, and I haven't seen her since she was a baby."

"You haven't?" Laura said in shock. "But she's your only family, your brother's child!"

His jaw clenched. "How could I see her?" he demanded, turning on her. "Why should I be allowed to spend time with my niece, when it was my thoughtless action that caused her to lose her father? Her grandparents? They never got to see her grow up. Why should I?"

"But, Gabriel...it was an accident. You were trying to help your brother. We all make mistakes with the people we love. Your brother would forgive you. Your family loved you. They would know your heart. They'd know you never meant to—"

"I'm done talking about this," he growled, raking his hair back with his hand. He set his jaw, and his dark eyes glittered. "You wanted to understand why I never want children. I've told you why."

She closed her eyes, drew a deep breath. Tears streamed down her face as she opened her eyes.

"It's too late," she whispered.

"What do you mean?" he demanded. "Too late? What are you saying?"

She lifted her chin. "I've never had another lover, Gabriel. How could I, when I never stopped loving you? It's always been you. Just you."

He stared at her. His dark eyebrows came together like a storm cloud. "That's impossible," he said angrily. "Robby—"

"Don't you understand?" She shook her head tearfully. "Robby is your son."

The echo of her words hung in the air between them like a noxious cloud.

Gabriel stared at her, then staggered back.

"What?" he choked out.

"Robby is your—"

"I heard you," he cried, putting his hands over his ears. But he couldn't stop his mind from repeating those words. *Robby is your son.* "You're wrong. It's impossible."

"No," Laura said quietly. "Didn't you notice how he looks so much like you? That he was born exactly nine months after our night together? How could you not know? How could you not see?"

He shook his head. "But—but it can't be," he gasped. "I was careful. I used protection."

She shook her head. "Condoms have been known to fail—"

"Only to people who use them incorrectly," he muttered. "I do not."

"But even then, three percent of the time they—"

"No." He held out his hand, blocking her words. He

felt as if he couldn't breathe, and loosened the tie on his tuxedo. "I can't be his father. I can't."

Laura took a deep breath. She looked so beautiful in her white gown and veil. He'd never seen her look so innocent, so beautiful. So deceitful.

"I know this must come as a shock to you," she said softly. She gave him a tremulous smile. "It was a shock for me, too. But Robby's not an accident. He's not a mistake."

"Then what is he?" Gabriel demanded.

She looked up at him, her blue eyes luminous.

"A miracle," she whispered.

Images of Robby's chubby, smiling face went through his mind. His dark hair, his inquisitive dark eyes. *Of course* Robby was his son. Pacing, Gabriel raked his hair back with his hand. How could he have not seen it before?

Because he hadn't wanted to see it, he thought grimly. Because having a child, when he'd killed his parents and prevented his brother from raising his, was the one thing he could not allow himself to do.

"I destroyed my own family," he said in a low voice, staring blindly through the windows toward the wintry hills. "I don't deserve another."

Laura came slowly toward him, her beautiful face filled with tenderness and love, her eyes glowing with light.

"What happened that night was an accident. It wasn't your fault. But you've buried yourself in the cemetery with them, not allowing yourself to be happy or loved, always punishing yourself—"

"Not punishment. *Justice*," he said in a low voice, feeling as if his heart were being ripped out of his chest. "If I hadn't tried to talk Guilherme out of having a family, if I hadn't tried to talk him out of committing to his wife and baby, they would all be alive. Why should I enjoy the life I denied my own brother?"

"Your brother is gone. He forgave you long ago. But we're still here, and we need you," she said. She took a deep breath and lifted her tearstained eyes to his. "Please, Gabriel. I love you. Love me back."

His jaw hardened as he stared down at her.

"Don't use the word *love*," he said harshly. "You lied to me. And you turned me into a liar, as well. I said I would never have a wife. Now look at me." Rage burned inside him as he gazed down at his tuxedo. He ripped the tiny rose boutonniere out of his lapel. "Just look at me!"

She went pale beneath her wedding veil, and the beautiful light in her eyes dimmed. "I'm sorry. It's why I didn't tell you I was pregnant. I knew it wasn't what you wanted, that you'd feel trapped by duty to a child. But—" she took a deep breath "—I couldn't marry you. Not without telling you the truth."

"Thank you," he said coldly, pacing the carpet. He stopped. His body felt chilled, as frozen as a New Hampshire winter. Maybe because of the icy dagger she'd just plunged through his back. "Thank you, Laura, for being so trustworthy and decent."

She flinched. Her eyes were red, her beautiful face swollen with tears. "I understand if you want to back out."

"Back out?"

"Of the wedding," she whispered.

He saw the way her petite, curvaceous body was shivering in her wedding dress. He forced himself not to care. What difference did her feelings make to him anymore? His lips curved as he looked at her scornfully. "I'm more determined to marry you now than ever."

She licked her lips and he saw a tremulous hope in her blue eyes. "Because you love Robby?"

He stared at her. "Because he's my duty."

Tears fell unchecked down her face as she clutched her arms together over her exquisite beaded gown. "Can't you even try to love him?"

"The deal stands," he said coldly. "I will still marry you. I will still take care of your son."

"*Our* son!"

For a long time, she stood, staring at him. Her lips parted to speak, and his cell phone rang in his pocket. Emotionlessly, he turned away from her. "Santos."

"I'm afraid I have to back out of our deal, Santos."

Gabriel recognized the voice at once. Felipe Oliveira. His eyes widened in shock as he stepped away from Laura. "Is that some kind of joke, Oliveira?" he growled into the phone. "Some attempt to drive up the price? Because you've already signed the papers."

"Just the preliminary papers. And Théo St. Raphaël has just offered me three million euros more for Açoazul than you. Best of all, he's throwing in his prize vineyard to sweeten the offer." The man gave a laugh. "I've always wanted to make my own champagne, and his vineyard is legendary."

"You can't do that!" Gabriel exploded. "We signed a contract!"

"A preliminary contract," the man pointed out gleefully. "All I need pay for reneging on the terms is a small penalty—a million American dollars. Which St. Raphaël has also offered to cover."

Gabriel cursed aloud. "But why? Why betray me like this, Oliveira, after we helped you see Adriana's true nature?"

The older man cackled. "Now that I'm rid of her, I suddenly find I'm interested in business again. Sorry, Santos." He paused, then said with greater seriousness, "Sorry, young man. But you'll live to fight another day."

"I'll leave within the hour," Gabriel said desperately. "I can be in Rio by tonight, and we can talk further—"

But Oliveira had hung up. Gabriel stared for a long moment at the phone in his hand. He felt dizzy with the vertigo of how much he'd lost in the last two minutes.

He'd lost...*everything*.

He whirled on Laura, who was staring up at him with big eyes. "Let's get the wedding over with," he growled, stomping toward the door. "As soon as it's over, we're leaving for Rio."

Her trembling voice stopped him. "No."

He frowned, looking back at her from the doorway. "No? What do you mean, no?"

She licked her lips, coming closer. Her eyes were luminous in the morning light.

"I could accept you not loving me," she said. "I told myself that my love could be enough for both of us." Her eyes narrowed, glittering like a frozen blue sea. "But I can't accept you not loving Robby. He can't just be your *duty*."

"I just found out he's my son," he retorted, "after a year of your lies. What do you expect from me? That I declare my love and fall at your feet?"

She looked at him, and her lips trembled in a smile. "That would be nice."

He shook his head angrily. "Accept what I can give you. And be grateful!"

"Grateful?" she cried. With an intake of breath, she held up the hem of her wedding dress and marched right up to him. Her beautiful face was outraged. "I waited five years for you to love me," she said. "I dreamed of you for the whole last year! All I wanted was for you to marry me..."

"And I will," he said impatiently. "Come on."

"But I was wrong." She lifted her chin. "Love is what matters. Without love, this marriage is nothing but a lie." She shook her head fiercely. "And I won't let Robby settle for that. I won't let him grow up wondering why his father doesn't love him, why his parents' marriage is so strained, what he's done wrong!"

Gabriel stared at her. It suddenly seemed as if an ocean divided them. He reached out his hand. "Laura..."

She slapped it away. "No!"

He glared at her. "I don't have time for this."

"So go."

He briefly considered the idea of dragging her forcibly down the aisle. But she was surrounded by farmers and ranchers and strong neighbors with guns, while to their eyes he was just some stranger who was taking her and Robby away.

But he wasn't just a stranger. He was Robby's father.

Gabriel sucked in a deep breath, overwhelmed by the flood of emotion in his heart. He couldn't give in to the feeling. *Couldn't...*

Grabbing her wrist, he started to pull her towards the door. "We will marry, then leave for Rio—"

She ripped her arm out of his grasp. "I'm not going."

"You're being ridiculous. Don't you understand? Oliveira is backing out of the contract! If I don't change his mind, I'll lose everything!"

"I understand," she said softly. "You should go."

"I'm not leaving the country without you and our son."

"I'm not marrying you. Not like this."

"You're being selfish!"

Laura swallowed, her cheeks pink. He could see he'd hurt her with the accusation. But she wasn't going to let him manipulate her so easily. "I'll never try to stop you from seeing Robby whenever you want. Our lawyers can work out some arrangement. But I won't marry you, and I won't leave the people who love us for someone who doesn't."

"So that's it?" he said incredulously. "You're giving me an ultimatum?"

"Yes." Her eyes filled with tears as she gave him a trembling smile. "I guess I am."

Gabriel swallowed against the sudden lump in his throat. He couldn't force her to marry him. He couldn't seduce or charm or bully her into it. When did she get so steady? When did she get so strong?

Raking his hair back, he looked at her. "Laura," he said slowly. He exhaled a deep breath. "I can't do it. What you're asking. I wish I could, but I can't. I can't… love you."

Pain flashed across her face, raw and sharp. Then she straightened her shoulders in her wedding gown.

Reaching up, she pulled the vintage lace veil off her elegant blonde chignon. Her blue eyes were stricken but steady.

"Then I'm sorry," she said quietly. "But if you can't love us…you can't have us."

CHAPTER FIFTEEN

GABRIEL had to hurry. Every second he wasted with Laura was like a grain of sand falling through a fatal hourglass. He had to leave at once.

And yet he couldn't.

Leaving her felt like a death. He took a deep, shuddering breath. "This isn't over," he said hoarsely. "I'll be back after I close the deal in Rio."

"Of course." Laura's shoulders straightened, even as her lower lip trembled. "I will never stop you from seeing Robby. I hope…I hope you'll see him often. He needs his father."

Gabriel heard the music start to play downstairs and thought of the guests surrounded by white roses and candlelight, waiting for the wedding ceremony to begin. He clenched his hands, feeling that same strange spinning, sinking feeling in the region of his chest.

"Remember," he said tersely, looking at her. "This was your choice. I wanted to marry you."

She swallowed as tears streamed unchecked down her pale cheeks. "I'll never forget that."

No, he thought suddenly. It couldn't end like this. Not like this!

With a sudden, ragged breath, he seized her in his

arms. Pressing his lips against hers, he kissed her with every ounce of passion and persuasion he possessed. He never wanted to let her go.

She was the one to pull away. He saw tears falling down her cheeks as she stepped back, out of his reach. "Goodbye."

He sucked in his breath. But there was nothing he could do. Nothing to be done. "I'll be back," he said heavily. "In a few days."

She gave him a wan smile. "Robby will be glad whenever you choose to visit."

He left the room. Went out the door. Walked past her mother, who was waiting at the bottom of the stairs. He went outside into the cold winter air to the limo waiting outside. Gabriel felt a sudden pain in his chest when he saw that someone—one of Laura's friends, perhaps—had written Just Married across the back window in white shaving cream, and attached aluminum cans to the back bumper to drag noisily down the road.

His hands clenched as he flung himself heavily into the backseat of the limo. Carlos, who'd apparently been texting someone as he waited in the driver's seat, jumped.

"Mr. Gabriel! What are you doing, so soon…? And where is Mrs. Laura?"

"She's not coming," he replied tightly. His throat hurt. "And she's not *Mrs.*"

"But *senhor*… What happened?"

Gabriel looked bleakly out the window, at the beautiful fields of endless white. "Just go."

Laura stood by the closed door until the sound of Gabriel's footsteps faded away.

Sagging into a chair, she covered her face with her hands. She'd been happy to be a bride, a single mother no longer—so pleased to finally leave the scandal behind her. She thought of her baby, downstairs now with one of her cousins, and a sob came from her lips.

But she'd had no other honorable choice. If she'd been willing to accept a life without love forever, what would that have done to her soul? What would that have taught her son?

She'd done the right thing. So why did she feel so awful?

She heard the door squeak open and looked up with an intake of breath.

Her three sisters, all dressed in elegant bridesmaid gowns, stood in the open door with their mother. "Why did Gabriel storm off like that?" Ruth asked tremulously. Then she saw Laura's tearful face. "Oh, sweetheart!"

A moment later, Laura was crying in their arms as they hugged her, and her scowling little sister Hattie was cursing and offering to go punch Gabriel in the face. That made Laura laugh, but the laughter turned to a sob. Wiping her eyes, she looked up at them.

"What do I do now?" she whispered.

Her mother searched her gaze. "The wedding is off? Is it for sure?"

Laura nodded with a lump in her throat. "He said he didn't love me, that he would never love me. Or Robby, either."

Her mother and sisters stared at her with a unified intake of breath. Then Ruth shook herself briskly.

"Well then. I'll go downstairs, tell everyone to head home."

Laura folded her arms, her belly sick with dread and

grief. "It'll cause such a scandal," she whispered. She stared at the patterns on the carpet as the full horror built inside her. "Just when all the rumors were coming to an end."

"Weddings get canceled all the time," Becky said staunchly. "There's nothing scandalous about it."

"Zero scandal," Hattie agreed quickly, pushing up her glasses. "It's totally uninteresting."

"Not even as interesting as when Mrs. Higgins's cow knocked over the Tast-E Burger truck," Margaret added.

"It'll be all right, sweetheart," her mother said, softly stroking Laura's hair as she sat beside her. "Just stay here. I'll handle everything."

It was very tempting. But with a deep breath, Laura shook her head.

"I'll ask your uncle, then," Ruth said quickly. "He's waiting to walk you down the aisle. He can simply make a little announcement and—"

"No," Laura choked out. "I did this," she whispered, rising to her feet. "I'll end it."

Climbing onto his private jet at the airport five miles away, Gabriel nearly bit the stewardess's head off when she offered him champagne. As she scurried off to the back cabin, he grabbed the entire bottle of Scotch from the galley and gulped straight from the bottle, desperate to feel the burn. But when he pulled the bottle from his lips, he realized the pain in his chest had only gotten worse.

It was his heart. His heart hurt.

"Ready, sir?" the pilot said over the intercom.

"Ready," Gabriel growled. Falling into the white

leather seat, he took another gulp of the bottle and stared out his window.

He felt as if he were leaving part of himself behind. His wife. His child.

Robby. His *son*. Gabriel still couldn't believe it.

He didn't want to go.

I have to, he told himself angrily. *I have no choice.* He remembered how his parents had taken Gabriel and Guilherme to visit the factories of Açoazul Steel. It had been truly a family company. His father had been president, his mother vice president of marketing. "Someday, boys," his father had said, "this company will be yours. Your legacy."

The jet's engine started. Closing his eyes, Gabriel leaned his head into his hands. He still remembered the sound of his father's laugh, the tender smile in his mother's eyes. They'd been so proud of their strong, handsome, smart sons. He could still hear his brother saying, at twenty years old, "I never intended to have a family so soon, but now I can't imagine it any other way. I'm happy, Gabriel. I am."

Grief gripped Gabriel's chest. Why hadn't he believed him? Why had he been so sure that *he* was right, and his brother wrong?

"Robby's not an accident. He's not a mistake."

He suddenly saw Laura's beautiful face as she'd stood in the morning light, wearing a wedding gown as luminescent as New England snow.

"Then what is he?"

She'd looked up at him. *"A miracle."*

He blinked, staring at the porthole window as the jet's roar increased. Last year, he'd let Laura go because he'd wanted her to find a man who could love her. He'd wanted her to be happy. He'd been so angry when he'd thought she'd thrown her dreams aside and fallen into bed with a man who didn't deserve her.

But she'd loved Gabriel himself all this time. She'd loved him without hope. She'd taken care of their baby all on her own, while carrying such a heavy weight on her shoulders at home. She'd assumed from the start that she and Robby were on their own.

Gabriel was the man who didn't deserve her.

He'd tried to offer her money. His name. But that wasn't what Laura wanted. She wanted his love. She wanted…a family.

Gabriel set down the bottle. His body felt hot and cold at once.

The jet lurched forward, taxiing toward the runway.

He gripped the armrests. He had to go back to Rio, or he'd lose his family's company forever. Açoazul SA would be dismantled. He would lose his last link to his family.

The jet started to go faster down the runway, and he sucked in his breath.

His family.

He'd told himself for twenty years that he didn't deserve another family. And yet, like a miracle, he had one.

He had a family. Right here and now. And he was choosing to leave them.

He sat up straight in his chair. His breathing came hard and fast. What about his family's legacy?

Legacy.

He had a sudden flashback of a million small memories of warmth and joy and home. Visiting the steel factory. Sitting on his father's shoulders at *Carnaval*, watching the parades go by. Vacations in Bahia. Dinner together each night. A life of love and tenderness. Until he'd made one dreadful mistake.

"Your brother would forgive you. Your family loved you," he heard Laura's warm, loving voice say. *"They would know your heart."*

The jet hit full throttle, racing down the runway faster and faster, preparing for takeoff.

And Gabriel suddenly realized he was about to make the worst mistake of his life. And this time it wouldn't be an accident, a car spun out of control on a rainy road by a nineteen-year-old boy. This time it would be a stupid, cowardly decision made by a full-grown man.

He hadn't wanted another family.

But he had one.

Gabriel saw the white fields fly past the window. The jet started to rise, lifting off from the ground, and he leapt to his feet with a scream.

"Stop!"

CHAPTER SIXTEEN

LAURA hesitated outside the closed doors of the huge, flower-strewn library, frightened out of her mind.

She could hear the rumble on the other side of door, the mutters and whispers. The wedding had been scheduled to start thirty minutes ago, and everyone was obviously starting to assume the worst.

But there was no way around it. She had to get through it. With a deep breath, she pushed the doors open.

The enormous two-story library had been modeled after an old English abbey with walls of gray stone. It was now festooned with white roses and candles, with hundreds of chairs set up to create an aisle down the middle.

At the sight of the bride standing at the end of the aisle, musicians hastily began to play "Jesu, Joy of Man's Desiring" on guitars and violins. Laura stopped the music with a chopping gesture across her neck.

Silence fell. She could have heard a pin drop as three hundred pairs of eyes turned to her.

She trembled, passing a hand over her eyes. Then she heard her baby cry out halfway down the aisle. Going swiftly to her cousin Sandy, who held him in her lap,

Laura took her son in her arms. Robby looked dapper in a little baby tuxedo just like his father's, complete with rose boutonniere. She smiled through her tears. For an instant, she just held her baby in her arms, feeling his soft skin and breathing his sweet smell.

Then, squaring her shoulders, she slowly turned to face her family and friends.

"Thank you all for coming," she said loudly, then faltered. "But I'm afraid… Afraid that…"

"What?" her great-aunt Gertrude demanded loudly from the back. "Talk louder!"

Laura's knees grew weak. Did she really have to announce to all her friends and relatives that the only man she'd ever loved had just left her at the altar? How had she ever thought this was a good idea?

"Did he leave?" one of her hotheaded cousins demanded, rising to his feet in the front row. "Did that man desert you?"

"No," she cried, holding up her hand. Even now, she couldn't bear for them to think badly of Gabriel. He'd always been honest with her from the beginning. She was the one who'd arrogantly tried to change him, who'd thought that if she loved him enough, he might love her back. She was the one who'd thought if he knew Robby was his son, he might change, and love the child he'd never wanted. "You don't understand," she whispered. "I told him to go. I made him leave—"

"You couldn't," a husky voice said behind her. "Though you tried."

With a gasp, she whirled around.

Gabriel stood in the double doorway, dark and dashing in his tuxedo. And most incredible of all, he was smiling at her, smiling with his whole face. Even his black eyes held endless colors of warmth and love.

"What are you doing here?" she murmured. "I thought you were gone."

He started walking toward her.

"I couldn't go," he said. "Not without telling you something."

"What?"

He stopped, halfway down the aisle.

"I love you," he said simply.

She swayed on her feet. She was dreaming. She had to be dreaming.

He caught her before she could fall. "I love you," he murmured with a smile, and he looked down at the baby between them. "And I love my son."

There was an audible gasp. Gabriel looked around him fiercely.

"Yes," he said sharply. "Robby is my child. Laura was afraid to tell me about Robby, afraid I wouldn't be able to measure up to be the man—the father—he needed." Gabriel looked back at her. "But I will. I will spend the rest of my life proving I can be the man you deserve."

A sob escaped Laura's lips. Reaching up, she put her hand to his cheek, looking up at him. "You love me?"

He pressed his hand over hers. She saw tears in his eyes. "Yes."

She blinked, sucking in her breath. "But what about the deal in Rio?"

He looked down at her. "I don't care about it. Let the Frenchman have it."

She gasped, shaking her head desperately. "But you've tried to get the company back all these years.

It's all you wanted. All you've dreamed about day and night!"

"Because I thought it was my family's legacy." He reached down to cup her cheek. A smile curved his sensual lips. "But it wasn't."

"It wasn't?" she whispered.

"My family loved me, and I loved them," he said. "No accident can ever change that. I will honor their memory for the rest of my life. I will honor them by living as best as I can until the day I die." He took her hand tightly in his own, looking down at her. "And today, I will start the rest of my life loving you."

"I love you…." she choked out. "So much." She swallowed, then shook her head. "But we can get married later. We should leave for Rio at once. I don't want you to lose your company, your family's legacy—"

"I haven't lost it. I've found it at last. My family's legacy is love," he said. "My family's legacy—" he lifted his shining eyes to her face "—is you."

The autumn leaves of New Hampshire were falling in a million shades of red, gold and green against the cold blue sky when Gabriel and Laura returned home from New York.

Laura sighed with pleasure as their SUV rounded the bend in the road and she caught her first glimpse of the old Olmstead mansion on the hill. It was the Santos house now. The day after their wedding, Gabriel had bought it for her as a present.

"It's too big," she'd protested. "We can't possibly fill all those rooms!"

He'd given her a sly, wicked smile. "We can try."

And they had certainly done their best. In fact, they'd

done excellent work on that front. Laura blushed. Since they'd moved into the house in March, they'd made love in all forty rooms, and also in the secret nooks of the large sprawling garden. They'd shared many warm evenings on the banks of their private lake, swimming and talking and watching the stars twinkle in the lazy summer night. One big pond, she thought, for what was sure to be one big family. She smiled. She would some-day teach her own children to swim there, as her father had taught her.

She'd been in New York City with Gabriel for only a single night, but she was already glad to be back home. She hadn't known it was possible for a man to fuss so much over his wife.

As the SUV stopped, she started to open the door, but Gabriel instantly gave her a hard glare. "Wait."

Laura sat back against her seat with a sigh.

He raced around the SUV and opened her door. Gabriel held out his hand, and his dark eyes softened as he looked down at her. She placed her hand in his, and felt the same shiver of love and longing that she had the very first time she'd touched his hand, in the days when she was only his secretary.

After helping her from the SUV—it wasn't as easy as it used to be—he closed the door behind her. He fol-lowed her constantly, anxiously, always concerned about her safety and comfort. It might have been irritating, if it wasn't so adorable.

"I can close my own door, you know," she observed.

He stroked her cheek, looking down at her fiercely. "I have a lot to make up for. I want to take care of you."

Glancing at the sweeping steps that led to the front

door, she lifted her eyebrow wickedly. "Want to carry me up the stairs?"

Grabbing her lapel, he pulled her against his dark wool coat. "Absolutely," he whispered, nuzzling her hair. He gave her a sensual smile. "Especially since the next flight of stairs leads straight to our bedroom."

Lowering his head to hers, he kissed her.

His lips were hot and soft against her own, and a contented sigh came from the back of Laura's throat. As he held her, a cold wind blew in from the north around them, scattering the fallen leaves and whispering of the deep frost that would soon come to the great north woods. But Laura felt warm down to her toes.

"You're a furnace," Gabriel said with a laugh as he pulled away. Then he smiled. "I think the baby is glad to be home."

"So am I," she said, then laughed. "For one thing, you won't be trying to throw yourself in front of trucks, trying to protect me on the crosswalk."

"Fifth Avenue is insane," he muttered.

"Yeah, all those crazed tourists and limo drivers," she teased. Turning, she started to walk toward the front steps. She was excited to see Robby, after his first overnight apart from them. He'd had two loving babysitters fighting over him, Grandma Ruth and nanny Maria. "Thanks for a lovely night. It was nice."

"Yeah." Lifting a dark eyebrow, he grinned wickedly, clearly remembering their time alone together in front of the fire last night.

She elbowed him in the ribs. "I meant with the girls."

"Right." He cleared his throat. "Your sisters seem to

be settling well. It's the first time I've seen them since they started college."

"You're not in New York very much these days," she teased.

"I have better things to do than work," he growled. "Like make love to my beautiful wife." Grabbing her again by the lapels of her warm camel-colored coat, he kissed her again, long and hard, before she pulled away.

"You are insatiable!"

He gave a dark, wicked grin. "I know."

A flash of heat went through her. After they'd married that blustery day in early March, he'd made love to her without protection for the first time. The sensation was so new to him that they hadn't left the bed for a full week after their wedding. In some ways, Laura thought, she'd been his first, just as he'd been hers. And they'd gotten pregnant on their honeymoon.

Laura put a hand on her jutting belly. Their baby, a little girl, was due in just a few weeks.

"Thanks for moving up here," she whispered. "I am so happy to be close to my family."

His eyes met hers. "So am I. And I have you to thank for that."

Maybe it was pregnancy hormones, but Laura still felt choked up every time she thought of the three girls now living in the same city, all going to college. Two of them were her sisters. Brainy Hattie had transferred to Columbia University, and eighteen-year-old Margaret had opted for NYU.

But the greatest miracle of all—Gabriel's young niece, Lola, was now at Barnard.

Last spring, shortly after Laura had found out she was

pregnant, she had tracked down Izadora, Lola's mother, and invited their family to come up for a weekend visit to New Hampshire in the private jet. To Gabriel's shock, they'd accepted.

After twenty years, Gabriel had finally made peace with Izadora and met her American husband, a restaurant owner in Miami. Gabriel had hugged his young niece for the first time since she was a baby. And he'd convinced Izadora to allow him to create a trust fund for Lola. "It's what Guilherme would have wanted," he'd said gravely, and put like that, how could Izadora refuse? Lola was now at Barnard College studying art.

"All this family around us." Wiping away her tears with a laugh, Laura shook her head and teased, "And you paying for three students at college already. Robby will probably want med school. And now this little one. Are you sure you're ready for more?"

Gabriel put his hands on her swelling belly beneath her long T-shirt. At nearly nine months along, she could no longer button her wool coat. Half the time she was too hot to wear it, anyway. "Just a few weeks now," he whispered. Dropping to one knee, he impulsively kissed her belly.

"Gabriel!" she gasped with a laugh, glancing up at the big windows of the house.

Her husband looked up at her. His eyes glowed with tenderness and love. "I'll be here this time, *querida*," he said in a low voice. "Every step of the way."

"I know," she said, her throat choking with tears of joy. Tugging him to his feet, she wrapped her arms around his neck and kissed him. And as the cold wind blew, carrying dry leaves down their long driveway, she felt only warmth and love in the fire of their embrace.

And Laura knew two things.

The fire between them would always last.

And second, that they had an excellent chance of filling all forty rooms.

REQUEST YOUR FREE BOOKS!

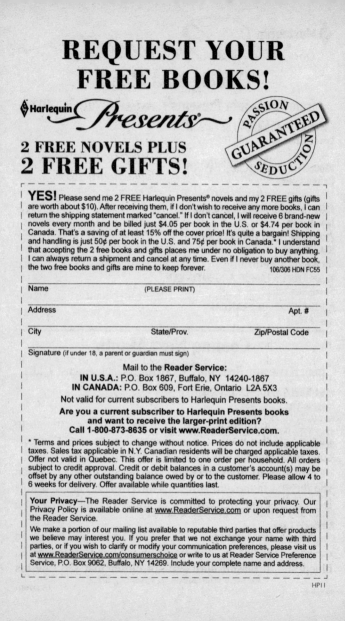

◆ Harlequin *Presents*

PASSION GUARANTEED SEDUCTION

2 FREE NOVELS PLUS
2 FREE GIFTS!

YES! Please send me 2 FREE Harlequin Presents® novels and my 2 FREE gifts (gifts are worth about $10). After receiving them, if I don't wish to receive any more books, I can return the shipping statement marked "cancel." If I don't cancel, I will receive 6 brand-new novels every month and be billed just $4.05 per book in the U.S. or $4.74 per book in Canada. That's a saving of at least 15% off the cover price! It's quite a bargain! Shipping and handling is just 50¢ per book in the U.S. and 75¢ per book in Canada.* I understand that accepting the 2 free books and gifts places me under no obligation to buy anything. I can always return a shipment and cancel at any time. Even if I never buy another book, the two free books and gifts are mine to keep forever.

106/306 HDN FC55

Name _____ (PLEASE PRINT)

Address _____ Apt. #

City _____ State/Prov. _____ Zip/Postal Code

Signature (if under 18, a parent or guardian must sign)

Mail to the **Reader Service:**
IN U.S.A.: P.O. Box 1867, Buffalo, NY 14240-1867
IN CANADA: P.O. Box 609, Fort Erie, Ontario L2A 5X3

Not valid for current subscribers to Harlequin Presents books.

**Are you a current subscriber to Harlequin Presents books
and want to receive the larger-print edition?
Call 1-800-873-8635 or visit www.ReaderService.com.**

* Terms and prices subject to change without notice. Prices do not include applicable taxes. Sales tax applicable in N.Y. Canadian residents will be charged applicable taxes. Offer not valid in Quebec. This offer is limited to one order per household. All orders subject to credit approval. Credit or debit balances in a customer's account(s) may be offset by any other outstanding balance owed by or to the customer. Please allow 4 to 6 weeks for delivery. Offer available while quantities last.

Your Privacy—The Reader Service is committed to protecting your privacy. Our Privacy Policy is available online at www.ReaderService.com or upon request from the Reader Service.

We make a portion of our mailing list available to reputable third parties that offer products we believe may interest you. If you prefer that we not exchange your name with third parties, or if you wish to clarify or modify your communication preferences, please visit us at www.ReaderService.com/consumerschoice or write to us at Reader Service Preference Service, P.O. Box 9062, Buffalo, NY 14269. Include your complete name and address.

HP11

*Once bitten, twice shy. That's Gabby Wade's motto—
especially when it comes to Adamson men.
And the moment she meets Jon Adamson her theory
is confirmed. But with each encounter a little something
sparks between them, making her wonder if she's been
too hasty to dismiss this one!*

*Enjoy this sneak peek from ONE GOOD REASON
by Sarah Mayberry, available August 2011
from Harlequin® Superromance®.*

Gabby Wade's heartbeat thumped in her ears as she marched to her office. She wanted to pretend it was because of her brisk pace returning from the file room, but she wasn't that good a liar.

Her heart was beating like a tom-tom because Jon Adamson had touched her. In a very male, very possessive way. She could still feel the heat of his big hand burning through the seat of her khakis as he'd steadied her on the ladder.

It had taken every ounce of self-control to tell him to unhand her. What she'd really wanted was to grab him by his shirt and, well, explore all those urges his touch had instantly brought to life.

While she might not like him, she was wise enough to understand that it wasn't always about liking the other person. Sometimes it was about pure animal attraction.

Refusing to think about it, she turned to work. When she'd typed in the wrong figures three times, Gabby admitted she was too tired and too distracted. Time to call it a day.

As she was leaving, she spied Jon at his workbench in the shop. His head was propped on his hand as he studied blueprints. It wasn't until she got closer that she saw his eyes were shut.

He looked oddly boyish. There was something innocent and unguarded in his expression. She felt a weakening in her resistance to him.

"Jon." She put her hand on his shoulder, intending to shake him awake. Instead, it rested there like a caress.

His eyes snapped open.

"You were asleep."

"No, I was, uh, visualizing something on this design." He gestured to the blueprint in front of him then rubbed his eyes.

That gesture dealt a bigger blow to her resistance. She realized it wasn't only animal attraction pulling them together. She took a step backward as if to get away from the knowledge.

She cleared her throat. "I'm heading off now."

He gave her a smile, and she could see his exhaustion.

"Yeah, I should, too." He stood and stretched. The hem of his T-shirt rose as he arched his back and she caught a flash of hard male belly. She looked away, but it was too late. Her mind had committed the image to permanent memory.

And suddenly she knew, for good or bad, she'd never look at Jon the same way again.

Find out what happens next in ONE GOOD REASON, available August 2011 from Harlequin® Superromance®!

Celebrating

Blaze™ **10** *years of*
red-hot reads

Featuring a special August author lineup of
six fan-favorite authors who have written
for Blaze™ from the beginning!

The Original Sexy Six:

Vicki Lewis Thompson
Tori Carrington
Kimberly Raye
Debbi Rawlins
Julie Leto
Jo Leigh

Pick up all six Blaze™
Special Collectors' Edition titles!

August 2011

Plus visit
HarlequinInsideRomance.com
and click on the Series Excitement Tab
for exclusive Blaze™ 10th Anniversary content!

www.Harlequin.com

HBCELEBRATE0811

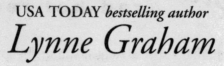

USA TODAY *bestselling author*

Lynne Graham

introduces her new Epic Duet

THE VOLAKIS VOW
A marriage made of secrets…

Tally Spencer, an ordinary girl with no experience of
relationships… Sander Volakis, an impossibly rich and
handsome Greek entrepreneur. Sander is expecting to
love her and leave her, but for Tally this is love at first
sight. Little does he know that Tally is expecting his
baby…and blackmailing him to marry her!

PART ONE:
THE MARRIAGE BETRAYAL
Available August 2011

PART TWO:
BRIDE FOR REAL
Available September 2011

Available only from Harlequin Presents®.

www.Harlequin.com

HPI3005